The Catnap Fumblers

book I

PRIVATE AFTERWORDS

J.B. THWAITE

Napuke Books

Ebook: ISBN 978-952-7600-00-9

Paperback: ISBN 978-952-7600-01-6

Hardcover: ISBN 978-952-7600-02-3

Book cover and illustrations: J.B. Thwaite aka Napukettu.

Publisher: Napuke, Finland (http://books.napuke.com)

Content information

Includes themes unsuitable for younger readers.
For a detailed list of potentially upsetting or triggering content, please visit
http://books.napuke.com.
There is a helpful glossary and cast of characters at the end of the book.

ARCTIC OCEAN
YAVELENG
AGNES POINT
EAREMOSS
THE WEAVER SEA
THE EAR OF THE CROWN
HERRING COVE
WHITSKERSEY
TASSKELD
SKIMOUTHKEY
PUFFINSBY
NISHKAWILLAT
NISHKAKARWAT MOUNTAIN RANGE
THE ARCTIC CIRCLE
INGENESS
THE NOKO SEA
RIMESVIK
GRUESHOLM
REIFSFELL
LINGSLIP
THRUSBY
TILLWICK
KANGFOSS
GNAST
TARTHWAITE
GREGLING
HIRMOUTH
QUITEMANY
HAITUWAT
HAMPIEDENPEHSEW
YARROWFELD
NISHKA
FORSTOFT
SKIFTON
LAKE UPERMERE
COWEMIRE
THE FOLDS
TORQUEA
EELTAWSAWTOO
PAYTOW
MINKHOLM
GOOPINGTON
YORKINGDALE
MIRRINBY
KIKBLOTCHAM
COORSAWS
WILTTY
BAERSKIRK
PELSBURY
COMBQUICK
WRENSBY
BULFFIELD
BLIP
TEWNEW
BRAMBLINGSHAW
BENTON HOUSE
CHILLWELL
PUSTLESTERSHIRE
THE REALM OF THE CROWN
FOXWICK
COPSETON
HARTFORD HEIGHTS
FUMBLETON
PITCHKIRK
DRIESBY
BRANTBY
TRUNKOSTER
MFFTHORPE
GROVESTEAD
SHRINKSTOFT
FIRTH
SNUTHMINSTER
GREAT HIDDING
GRYMSWICH
HOODMINSTER
LESSER HIDDLING
MOISTWICH
GLIBSTING
BLISSTERING
SHAFTINGSHEAD
GROUSEDALE
GOBEHURST
THE FURUYAN
CHATTSMOUTH
STUMBLENESS
DAMPKIRK
ASSMORE
SCHADESBOROUGH
CUMBERING
FURNESS
LANGPHLEGMINTON
SWETSHAMSHIRE
STOATNESS
CHESTCHESTER
SHREWSTER
RUYAN OCEAN
BOOTSLICKING
BRUNFALLOW
THE EAST SEA
CALADH NAN SGROTHACH
BRÀIGH NA BÈISTE
FURUYAN
IN THE YEAR 1890
MÙRAICH GAINMHICH
LÀIRIG ÀIR
SCALE
PORT MU DHEIREADH
GRÒM
THE FOOTSTEPS
BASENYETT PROJECTION
N
W
E
S

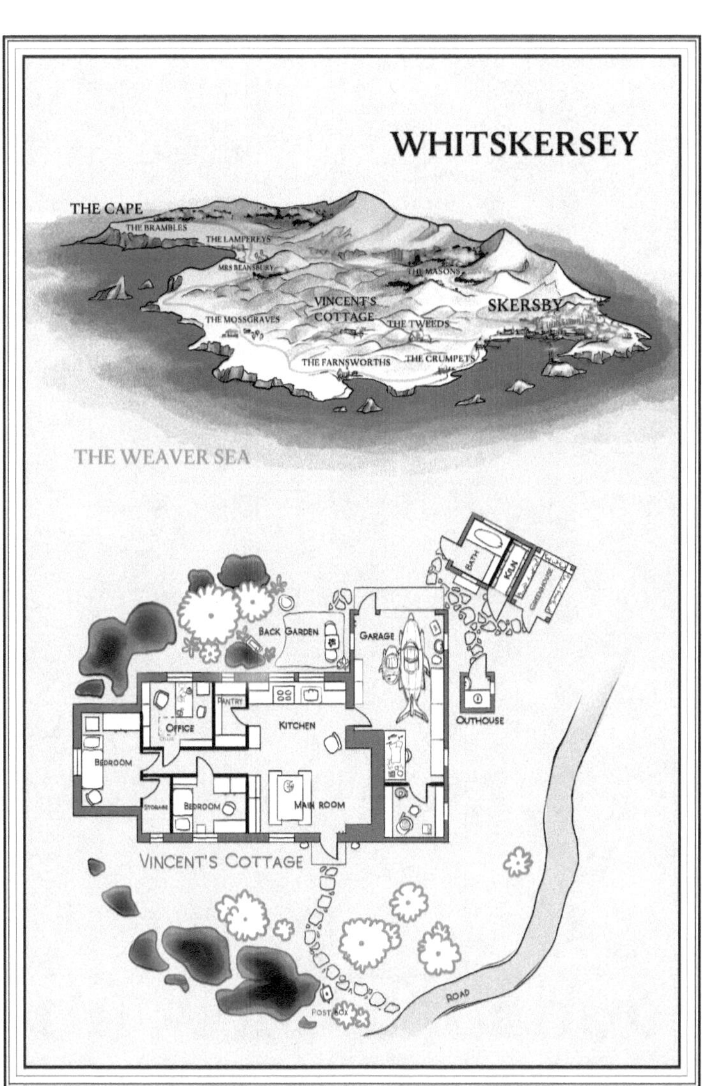

WHITSKERSEY
THE CAPE
THE BRAMBLES
THE LAMPREYS
MRS BEANSBURY
THE MASONS
VINCENT'S COTTAGE
SKERSBY
THE MOSSGRAVES
THE TWEEDS
THE FARNSWORTHS
THE CRUMPETS
THE WEAVER SEA
BATH
KGN
GREENHOUSE
BACK GARDEN
GARAGE
OUTHOUSE
OFFICE
PANTRY
KITCHEN
BEDROOM
STORAGE
BEDROOM
MAIN ROOM
VINCENT'S COTTAGE
POST BOX
ROAD

THE CITY OF
SCHADESBOROUGH

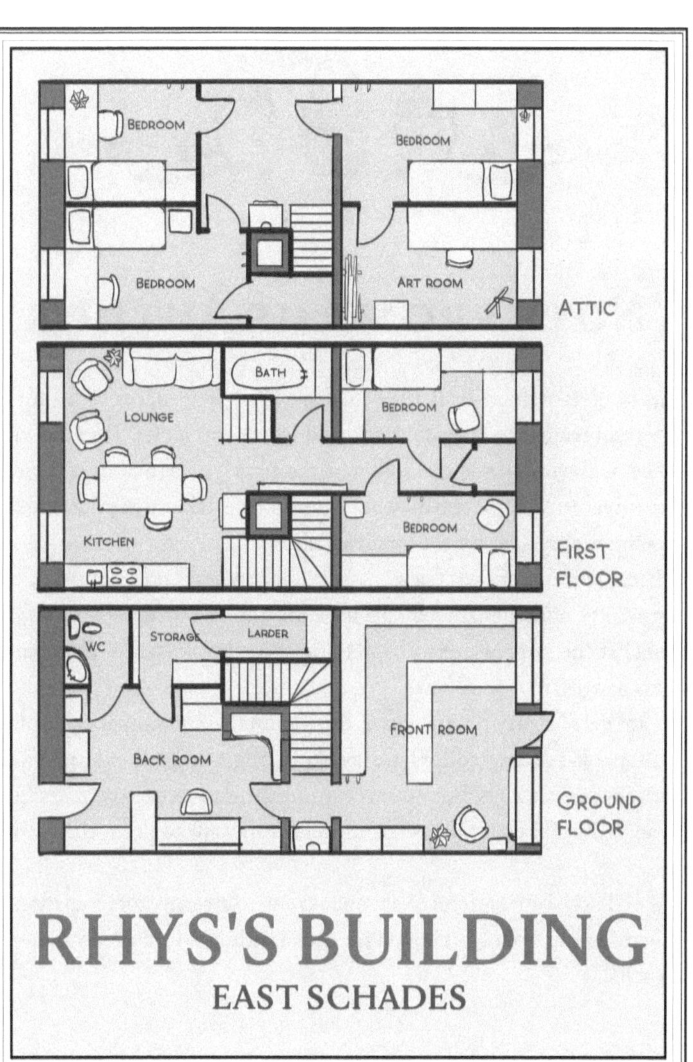

RHYS'S BUILDING

EAST SCHADES

Note from the Author

This book is written in British English. Here is a bucket of z's for my American readers to take along and add where you see fit. Take the whole bucket with you, so you can collect all the extra letters (mainly u's) into it. You can return it at the end of your read, and I will take care of the recycling. I ~~apologise~~ apologize for the inconvenience!

Because this story has fairly many points of view and a couple of time jumps, I've added character-specific dinkuses (the decorative thingamabobs) at the start of every chapter and scene break (where the point of view changes) to clue you in.

I am deeply sorry for any typos, extra commas or grammatical mistakes in this book. I and my editor have been on a lengthy expedition to hunt and catch the pesky things, but we are only human, and some may have slipped through. My inbox is always open should you want to point them out to me.

And lastly, I am grateful to anyone willing to give my story a chance. It's something I've been working on for over a decade, so I sincerely hope you enjoy it!

DEDICATIONS

This novella is dedicated to all the courageous souls who jumped into the unknown and gave my debut trilogy a chance.

And if you haven't read the full Catnap Ramblers trilogy before picking up this novella, this is your last warning to turn back, do yourself a favour and read it first!

Chapter 1

On the arctic island of Whitskersey, the slight increase in daylight roused gently the sleeping creatures and plantlife after months of winter darkness. The tough, weather-worn trees and bushes pushed out their tiny buds despite the continuing cold nights and chilly winds. Last year's browned grass, lichen and moss formed a colourful blanket now springing to life where packed snow had covered it only days prior.

Vincent parked the speeder at the front yard of the cottage instead of taking it to the garage. Ren turned to look at him, questioningly.

"I thought I'd drop the three of you off here, so you don't need to wade through the mess." If memory served, he'd left a few things lying around after fixing the speeder and preparing to go last year, and it wasn't exactly the first impression he wanted to make. "Do you mind checking the post box for me? I have a feeling it might be full."

Vincent helped Ren down from the cockpit and she, in turn, helped Jasmine from the sidecar.

Aurora had already stepped off on her own and was stretching herself and looking around the front yard. There wasn't much to see since they hadn't had time to replant any of the trees that had burned down in the fire. Only one of them was left standing.

"It's lovely." She turned to look at Vincent, smiled and made Vincent's poor heart skip a beat. She'd always had this effect on him, but for whatever reason, it seemed to be only getting worse.

Vincent cleared his throat.

"I'll go park this thing. Ren will show you inside."

"Yes! Right this way!" Ren had retrieved a lap full of postcards and letters and was already running to the front door.

Julian's Automatic Rest Facilitator mask was in place, so he lay within his bubble, peaceful and unmoving. Rhys had spent an embarrassing number of nights just sitting here next to him.

After everything that had happened, resting in Julian's presence dreamside, even with him unaware, was more relaxing than having to sleep alone. His bubble was cosy, and Rhys felt safe confined here, as if he were sitting within a protective cocoon.

It had felt more of an invasion of privacy to read through Julian's medical files when his mother had brought them to the pharmacy, even when Julian had given them permission to do so. Together with Hosta and Vera, they had come up with some ideas on what to try in order to fix some of what was wrong with Julian. However, after a lengthy discussion with Hosta about the details of the treatments they had already tried on the twins, it was clear they wouldn't be able to fix everything.

Combing through Julian's files and data and comparing them with Vincent's, Vera had confirmed Mrs Craft's claim that she'd never intended to harm her children. It seemed the bulk of the issues plaguing Julian even today had been there since birth. The way his mother had gone about trying to help remained somewhat suspect, but at least she'd openly admitted to implementing a few superfluous changes to ensure Julian's cooperation during his treatment and surrendered these details willingly in an effort to help.

Vincent at least seemed to be on the mend after his breakthrough with sleep this past Midwinter's Eve and was reportedly doing much better even without the medication. One less thing for Rhys to worry about.

Since there was no way to fully remedy the rambly issue Julian had dreamside, Rhys had put off trying. Julian had leaned towards not wanting him to try because of the danger the uncontrollable temper posed here, but he'd said he would cooperate if Rhys decided it was worth the risk. It was difficult to say whether the man was disappointed about them not giving a go, but it had seemed like he might have been at least a smidge sad about it.

Rhys had the whole night to consider whether to postpone this again like he'd done the past dozen or so nights.

The problem was he wanted to have everything: he wanted to enjoy this calm but also to hear Julian's unfiltered thoughts. He wanted Julian to feel comfortable here without the fear of oversharing. He wanted the excitement sans the anxiety, and it was impossible to decide which of the options he preferred the most.

He leaned over Julian to inspect the mask again and what he suspected were the damaged parts of Julian's brain. Whether it was Hosta's treatments, Julian's past drinking and drug abuse or a birth defect, something had left behind what looked like dozens of partially scarred, half-healed lesions across his dreamside form. Without a healthy model to compare to, Rhys was worried he might poke and break something without realising.

Since some of it was visibly intentional, and Hosta and Vera had briefed him on what to look for, Rhys could try to do something about the most obvious areas... whether that was enough to make a difference remained unclear. If it failed, Julian would have to remain ARF'ed until they could come up with something better.

Rhys took a few, deep, calming breaths and removed the ARF mask.

Julian frowned.

"I'd like a sandwich," he said, sat up and opened his eyes.

"What?"

"A sandwich… Oh, hello Rhys." Julian blinked. "Where did Quin go?"

"You had a dream about Quin?"

"Yes, you and Quin…" He sat up and looked around himself. "Oh, I thought I woke up. I guess not. Did you make your decision? Are you feeling up for it? Are we doing something tonight?"

"Yes, but first, what sort of a dream?" Rhys was intrigued.

Julian bit a knuckle to stop himself. Evidently he didn't want to share.

"Fine, you don't have to tell me." Rhys sighed. "I need you to visualise something for me and then change that part about yourself. I'm going to guide you through it."

Rhys sat behind Julian and placed both of their hands on Julian's scalp. This was probably not strictly necessary, but it made it feel more intuitive and easier to explain because Julian might struggle to visualise his insides and, lacking sensation within his brain, wouldn't have been able to feel exactly where Rhys's hand was.

"I need you to let your fingers drift through as if there were nothing in the way. It may take a moment before you get the hang of it but just relax and let my hand guide you." Rhys pushed Julian's fingers gently until they eased through his skull.

Rhys was accustomed to moving through objects dreamside, but the sensation of sticking one's fingers freely into a person's brain was likely as disturbing for Julian as it had been for Rhys the first time he'd tried it with Hosta. It still gave him the willies.

"Can you feel this part?"

Julian grunted.

"What are you doing? That doesn't feel right."

"Vera explained this should be smooth, and there should be no gap here." Rhys indicated the respective parts he wanted Julian to concentrate on.

"What am I supposed to do about it?"

"Imagine this is smooth." Rhys moved Julian's fingers across a deep lesion and waited. There was a slight improvement. "A little more," he instructed, "and then these edges should align."

"I could have already fixed this long ago, just by sticking my fingers in there and imagining it?" Julian sounded annoyed, but he was making the changes. "Will it stick?"

"We're hoping. Does it feel any different?"

"I can't tell. I'm afraid to wait and find out." Julian was still biting his finger between replies, just in case.

"Well, let's do a few more. These deliberate-looking ones are probably the source of your rambling, so even if your temper doesn't improve, at least you should have some more control over your output."

Rhys helped Julian with a few more bits. The repairs were better than expected, but from what he knew and could tell by comparing himself, Hosta and Julian, there were some parts that were too far gone to do anything about. Too much of the information was missing.

"Let's try this out." Rhys removed Julian's finger from his mouth. "Tell me more about the dream you just had. What was it about?"

Julian looked like he was struggling but kept his mouth shut.

"That should spare your extremities from the worst of it," Rhys said, a little disappointed.

"Not by much."

"Is it difficult?"

"Yes..." Julian sighed. "It feels crowded in my head. A lot of thoughts, but I can hold them in if I concentrate."

"I'm sorry. I don't know what else to try... Maybe this part?"

"What do I do with it?"

"Ever so slightly to the left, maybe. Less. And this area seems like it might be a bit rough. Did it help?"

"I'm not sure."

"Do you want me apply the ARF for you again so you can go back to your dream?"

"No. Let's see how well I can manage." Julian turned to face Rhys. "It's been a while since we did this. I thought you'd decided it wasn't worth it."

"I was just nervous," Rhys admitted. "I didn't want to get your hopes up, and also—" Rhys cleared his throat. "After what happened, I've not been feeling myself."

"Oh? How bad is it?"

Rhys thought about it.

The issue of not being able to tell whether he was awake or not had resolved itself quickly, but the nightmares were still ongoing. They'd removed his mask in less than a week when he'd no longer refused to sleep and rest regularly, but that hadn't meant things had gone back to normal.

He hadn't slipped between dream states by accident these past few days, but his senses were not as keen as he was used to. He felt as though he'd been ill for a long time and thus out of shape.

Asleep, he would sometimes forget where he was and what he was doing, although, as soon as he stopped to think about it, he had no trouble telling what was what. Those few seconds still left him feeling panicky for a while, though. It was why he preferred to rest in Julian's bubble instead of his own vast, open space.

"Not bad at all anymore. I just don't feel quite myself yet. I'm sure it'll pass."

"Ah, good. I was worried." Julian exhaled.

The conversation felt normal. Almost exactly like when they were awake. If Julian was struggling with his rampant thoughts, it certainly no longer showed. To Rhys, he looked as good as cured.

"Well, I'm fine now. And you seem to be doing better as well." Rhys was happy that they'd done so well, but now that they were conversing normally again, everything was brought to a standstill. It seemed just as difficult to initiate anything here as when they were awake.

Hold up—! Rhys interrupted himself. Initiate what? What was he hoping to do exactly? Kiss and fool around like the handful of times before? That seemed so far off in the past, and with everything that had happened in between, he wondered if he'd been so sleep-deprived back then that he'd dreamt it all without realising.

Maybe this conversation was bland and boring because it had always been like that?

"Why do you look so serious? Are you sure you're fine?" Julian asked.

Ah, crap, he'd forgotten to smile.

"Probably. I just realised I have some trouble remembering everything that has happened in the past month or so." Rhys laughed, hoping to lighten the mood.

"You were pretty out of it, so I'm not surprised. Anything in particular? Maybe I can help."

"I'm uh, generally a little hazy on some of the... details. It's fine. I'm sure it's not that important." Rhys scrambled to think of something benign to change the subject to. "So, did you have anything you wanted to do while we're here?"

"I want to touch your naked body, feel you against my skin and kiss you until it has driven me to the edge of my sanity," Julian said, realised what he'd said and stopped to rub the bridge of his nose. "I mean, just chatting with you is fine. I got a little distracted. Did you know you have... you have..." He leaned closer. "You have a birthmark, or is that a freckle? What is that...? Here... May I?" He touched Rhys's left cheek.

"It's a birthmark." Rhys was caught off guard by both Julian's reply and his touch. He held his breath while Julian inspected his face.

"Would you mind if I kissed you?" Julian asked.

Rhys swallowed. Had he really dreamt the previous times and none of it had actually happened? Why was Julian asking so politely? He seemed to be waiting for an answer, too, so it must have not been a rhetorical question.

"I don't mind."

As soon as Rhys had said it, he could feel Julian's lips against his own. He was fairly sure he'd felt this before. He realised he'd missed it.

"Can we do more, I need something more," Julian whispered. He sounded somewhat childish when he said it, but he was much more in control of himself than before.

"What would you like?" Rhys asked before he realised it would likely be construed as an invitation for an actual request and not just curiosity.

"Everything," Julian said before he returned to nibbling on Rhys's lips as if sampling their taste.

Rhys wondered if Julian would ever be as open with him awake as he was now. Would he express his wants and needs this freely?

"That's going to take a while." Everything was a broad concept, after all.

"You speak as though you were willing to give it to me."

When Julian looked Rhys in the eye, it was difficult to look away but also to keep looking. Rhys swallowed.

"Not everything," he corrected hastily.

"Everything besides *that*?" Julian asked.

"Everything but—" Rhys began. "No, wait, what's everything? What does that entail? What do I need to do?"

"Maybe it's easiest if you tell me to stop if you don't like it," Julian said. It sounded simple enough. How bad could it be?

"All right," Rhys agreed warily. He wondered if Julian had really gained enough self-control to restrain himself if needed but didn't have much time to worry about it before his attention was turned to Julian's mouth not only on his lips but on his neck and chest once he'd ripped open the shirt and pushed Rhys back to lie down on the floor.

Rhys shivered. He'd been aroused before, but the sensation he experienced now was novel. What was this? It was definitely not the same. It was nuanced, specific and subtle; not the sort of general, all-encompassing pleasurable feeling as when it had spilled over from Julian before.

Julian looked up from what he was doing. "Is something wrong?" he asked.

"N-no..." Not wrong per se but different and just the tiniest bit unsettling.

"You look like there is." Julian leaned back on his hands and hovered over Rhys, waiting.

"I— I don't know, it feels weird." Rhys wasn't sure how to describe it.

"Bad?"

"No..." Rhys watched Julian return to kissing his abdomen and waist.

Where was that almost uncomfortable heat from before? Was it because Julian was so much calmer than before, and if so, was it not as fun for h—?

Rhys's thought was cut short so abruptly, he lost track of it. A sharp, hot wave flashed through him and for a moment he forgot how to breathe.

"Sorry, did you feel that?" Julian looked up again.

"What was that?" Rhys steadied his breathing.

"I got distracted," Julian said, a little sheepishly. He loosened the top of Rhys's underwear and continued what he was doing.

The subtle sensation was back, but it was more defined than before. It took Rhys a few more minutes to identify it, but when he did, his face turned bright red.

"A—!" Shit, it was an erection?! Was it? Was it really? He stared as Julian pulled down his pants. It was indeed hard. Why? How? What...?! Julian wrapped his lips around it.

"A-a-a-aaah!"

Rhys wanted to grasp onto something to keep still, but there was nothing at his reach.

Shiiit, that thing was sensitive! It had become stiff once or twice before, but it had never felt like this. Why did it feel like this? Rhys let out a low, deep and oddly relaxed groan. Julian looked up but didn't let go. Rhys could feel the man's tongue stroking him firmly.

"Ffffff— Aaahh!" What the hell sort of black magic bullshit was this? It felt so good! He could have had this sooner, maybe, if he'd thought to ask? "More.... More, ahh... more..." Rhys could not stop himself. As he made noise, Julian got distracted again. After a few of these distractions, he let go to catch his breath.

"Don't stop—!" Rhys had been left hanging enough times to fear it might happen again.

"Rhys, please..." Julian closed his eyes for a moment. "I'm going to continue, don't worry, I just need a moment. You sound so..."

There was that heat again for a moment until Julian pulled himself back together. When he continued, Rhys tried to not make as much noise, but it was no use. The throbbing sensation was too distracting, and he couldn't resist the temptation of causing Julian to lose his grip by letting the moans out.

"Ah... don't you, ahhh, fucking dare— ahhh, to stop!" It was almost painful, it felt so good. "Juliannnn..." Rhys hung in there for as long as he could, but he could feel he was about to lose it.

He would have tried to be more considerate about it, had he been more experienced, but he didn't know exactly what to expect, even if he knew the gist. When he started to cum, he was surprised he was even capable of it. He'd never imagined he could but wondered if it had something to do with him being here, and Julian knowing first hand what this felt like.

Once Rhys was spent, he lay there in a state of lingering euphoria. He'd never even dared to dream he could feel like this, that it was something that could happen to him.

"You didn't stop me, so I take it you liked it?" Julian climbed on top of him and snuggled against his neck.

"Uh huh." Rhys didn't know what to say. What was there to say after something like that?

"You smell good. I'm tired..." Julian mumbled. Rhys looked him in the eye, a little worried. "Tired of having to keep myself in check. I just want to..." Julian breathed raggedly. The air became hot and heavy. "I want to...

I want..." He looked almost pitiful in the state he was in. Rhys gave him a soft kiss.

"What do you want?" He smiled at Julian. Julian responded with another kiss.

"I want everything." He squeezed Rhys so tightly he had difficulty breathing.

"I know, I know." Rhys chuckled. "I'll give you anything you want."

CHAPTER 2

"Julian, I think I need your help." Rhys had been feeling distinctly odd since supper. He'd retired into his room to read but soon realised it was getting worse. There was no way he was going to be able to sleep like this.

Julian had been working at his desk in the back room as usual but hadn't been so engrossed as to not look up from his work when Rhys came down the stairs.

"What is it? Can't sleep?"

"No, I'm not feeling right." There had been several reasons to not feel right as of late, but this was a new one.

There had already been a hint of something strange when he'd woken up this morning, but it wasn't until the glass of wine at supper that he'd relaxed and become aware of it.

"I can give you the usual dose." Julian reached for his kit.

"No, not like that. I don't mean— that's not what—" It was going to be tricky to explain this one.

"What is it? Do you feel sick? Is it the wine?" Julian looked worried.

"No..." He'd drunk more than a glass to distract himself from the sensation and to power through the meal, but he was barely drunk enough to brave this conversation, so it would have taken much more to feel sick because of it. "Do you perhaps have something like a numbing cream or salve or such I could use?"

"Did you hurt yourself? Maybe a cold compress—?"

"No..." Rhys sighed.

With Julian's pedantry, he would probably request details until he reached a solid diagnosis and could decide on the most appropriate treatment. He was waiting. Maybe the cold compress wasn't such a bad idea.

"Are you lonely? Do you need me to come sleep with you?"

Rhys tried to steer his mind out of the gutter, but his mind was more of a steam train travelling on a track, not a boat, bicycle or an automobile. Julian had probably meant it as a simple offer to keep him company until he fell asleep because that's what he'd done almost every night when Rhys had been ARF'ed dreamside and unnerved by falling asleep alone, but Rhys's mind was hoping to take it less literally.

With last night's pleasurable experience fresh on his mind, the uncomfortable pressure in the offending area he was ignoring with the persistence of a salmon swimming upstream was only getting worse.

Maybe a cold compress and the usual dose, as well as telling Julian to hurry up and go to bed would do the trick...

"I can't help you unless you tell me what's wrong." Julian's hand moved to Rhys's waist in a likely casual offering of support. He looked much less stern when he was seated and looking up at Rhys. His features had never looked as handsome and his lips as inviting. Why did he look this attractive all of a sudden?

Maybe a massage might help.

"Is it a fever?" Julian reached to test Rhys's forehead. That hand had touched him so many times, it shouldn't have made a difference, but last night... Rhys held his breath.

"It's not a fever." How could it feel this uncomfortable while making him yearn for more? He leaned on Julian, pulled him closer against his chest and wrapped his arms around Julian's head.

"It's hurting down there," Rhys admitted with a whisper. "Can you do something to relieve it..."

"It hurts?"

"—so bad it hurts... I want you so bad."

Julian squeezed him and pulled him to sit on his lap.

"What do you want me to do?"

"I'm not sure..." Another night dreamside might do more harm than good since he'd woken up with this condition. "You might... You might have to..."

Julian waited patiently for Rhys to finish, but, before too long, he improved his hold and lifted Rhys off to carry him upstairs.

For once, Rhys hadn't the will to resent the ease with which Julian was carrying him. There was a sense of safety being held this tightly while being carried off like invaluable treasure. Maybe it would be all right. Maybe it wouldn't be as bad as he feared. Maybe Julian would know what to do.

Julian lowered Rhys into bed and gave him a kiss.

"Are you sure about this? Do you need something? More wine?" Julian suggested.

"No, it's fine." His heart was beating in a frenzy, but even if it could have been calmed with more wine, or he might have become less aware if he were drunk out of his mind, it was not going to solve his problem.

Rhys didn't want to forget what had happened the night before. Julian was not going to become magically less attractive any time soon, so Rhys's body would probably respond the way it did until they both became shrivelled and old. He did not fancy becoming an alcoholic until then.

"Tell me to stop if it doesn't feel good."

"What will you do?"

"The same thing as last night. Don't think about it. It's essentially the same."

Julian gave him another kiss. It made Rhys throb from the anticipation and dread. His instincts screamed it wasn't going to be the same at all, but Julian's words repeated in his mind like a reassuring spell.

Julian removed Rhys's breeches much too swiftly. Rhys extended his hand to try to slow him down, but things were already visible down there, and the thought of everything being exposed made him well up. He bit his teeth together and shielded his eyes with his forearm.

"I told you to tell me to stop." Julian's voice was gentle. He had crawled closer to Rhys's ear. He moved Rhys's arm aside and kissed his tears away like a goddamn courting gentleman.

"Stop that." Rhys shoved him off.

"Yes, like that." Julian chuckled. "That's what you're supposed to do."

Rhys dished him a brief glare, even if he was incredibly grateful for the way Julian had just disarmed the situation.

"May I?" Julian set his hand on Rhys's thigh.

Rhys braced himself and nodded.

"I'm not going to put anything in there. Don't worry." Julian massaged the side of the thing frustratingly gently. It was only making it worse.

"I need you to do it like it's a muscle that's cramping." Or harder than that... Can you just massage it all off, Rhys thought, out of habit.

"It's not a muscle cramp," Julian said.

"But regardless, that's just making it more frustra—" Rhys was interrupted by a gasp he only just managed to hold in. What the bloody fucking shit was that?

Julian raised his eyebrows.

"I gather you haven't explored this much on your own."

Rhys shook his head in haste.

"I'll start doing it by hand until you're used to it." Julian continued to massage it softly.

What good was that going to do? It didn't seem like that part of it would do anything. At least Julian was offering him a kiss as a welcome distraction. Anything to get his mind off of the uncomfortable pressure.

Some minutes into it, Rhys was struggling to breathe. He didn't want to make noise with Quin and Victor still in the house, but it was difficult to keep his breath both silent and steady.

"It would be easier if we loosened this up a little." Julian gestured at the front of Rhys's shirt.

"Absolutely not—!" The gut instinct kicked in.

The binder felt more restrictive than usual, but even if Julian had already seen what was under it, and Rhys didn't wear the thing every day anymore, it was like an essential protective shield he was unwilling to part with.

"All right. Well, let me know if you change your mind."

Julian resumed.

Rhys felt dizzy... but wasn't it a bit too soon to change his mind? Most of his concentration was going into breathing. He was reminded of Quin's weird infatuation with asphyxiation, and it made even less sense to him.

"It's not supposed to be a punishment, Rhys." Julian stopped to open the front of Rhys's shirt to loosen the binder. "I'll leave your chest covered."

Ah, it instantly felt much, much better. Rhys drew a deep breath and relaxed. Once he found he could relax, it felt much more like the night before. He instinctively reached to grab Julian by the neck to kiss him. The pressure was back. It was definitely getting worse. Julian's hand was making it worse. It was absolutely awful.

"A—" Rhys bit his lip.

"Too fast? You need me to slow down?"

No, no, no, hell no. More. He was aching for more, but it was all wrong. It wasn't the same at all. Rhys couldn't say a word. He only stared at Julian, hoping the man would do something to make it better somehow.

"Not slower? You want more?"

What? Was it written on his face, or had he spoken out loud without realising? He clamped his mouth shut to not make noise as Julian proceeded to massage his dishonourables.

"You need to breathe, though." Julian stopped again.

"I'm breathing, I'm breathing." Rhys tried to kiss him to hurry him along but more so as a desperately needed source of distraction from the building heat.

"It's more challenging when you keep kissing me." Julian smiled at him. "I'll do it like last night. It'll feel better that way."

When Rhys watched him move lower down, the view was not the same at all. He looked away but couldn't get it out of his mind. He stretched his arm out to stop Julian.

"No?" Julian asked.

Rhys swallowed and fumbled in his confusion.

It didn't look the same, but would it feel the same? Would it feel any good? Would it help make this feeling go away?

He looked down and moved his hand aside. Julian was about to resume, but Rhys couldn't bear it and stopped him again.

With all of this indecisive waffling, Julian was bound to grow tired of him. Surely, the man was already getting impatient having to deal with a heap of weeping garbage!

"I'm sorry," Rhys cried. "It's annoying, isn't it? You don't have to care, just do it and get it over with…"

"There's no hurry on my account." Julian inched himself back next to Rhys. "I'll kiss you for as long as you need to forget about it."

Oh, right. This was not the dreamside, and Julian was more himself. Even if he wasn't exactly renowned for his patience or temper, this much might still be fine. Rhys exhaled. No need to panic, he reminded himself.

"I think I might need that glass of wine after all…" Maybe if he went through with this once, however he managed it, it would be easier next time?

"If you really want. But you're doing fine. We're really not in a hurry."

It might have been much easier to get entirely puffin-brained for a half-crown and throw himself into it with drunken abandon, but when Julian was being this patient and kind, it was nigh impossible to tune it out and let things run their course. He was treating Rhys so delicately and being so accommodating, it was starting to feel special, like a Guardian damned wedding night!

Julian's hand was cradling the unmentionables between Rhys's thighs, as if ever-so-gently inviting them to react.

Rhys closed his eyes. If only he could have been entirely honest with himself and admitted it felt good… He could almost forget that he was awake. Almost.

"Remember how I sucked on it last night? I'd like to do that again. Put the length of it in my mouth and swallow—"

Rhys opened his eyes to Julian's face in front of him, grinning.

"I can almost taste it." The man leaned in for a kiss. "It's still there. It's just inside of you. I'd like to dig it out with my tongue."

Rhys gasped from the words and the finger digging into the soft of his flesh. Hadn't he said he wasn't going to put anything in? He'd promised not to! Rhys was about to panic when he realised the fingers stopped well short of entering. They were only applying some pressure on the thing that now felt like it was pulsating under it.

"A… Ju—"

"Does it feel good?"

"Uh, ah—" His whole lower half was throbbing ominously.

"I'm not going to put anything in there unless you ask me to, but this much is fine, right?" With his palm massaging the front, he moved his fingers. It sent a pleasurable shiver through Rhys's spine. "Would you like this to be my tongue?"

With a fresh reference in his mind of how Julian's mouth had felt against his dick, Rhys shivered again. Yes. Oh, Lord yes.

"I'd like to hear you say it, so I don't misunderstand. But it definitely looks as though you'd enjoy it." Julian's grin was aggravatingly handsome.

Rhys wondered what had been in that wine to make him feel so intoxicated by the sight. Damnit if that face didn't make him want to eat the man alive.

"I'd like it," Rhys whispered, but he wasn't at all confident he could handle it.

Julian reassumed his position lower down, and while the view wasn't the same, the eyes looking up at Rhys were as soft and reassuring.

"Aa— fff—!" Rhys caught himself just in time to not outright moan. Julian gave him a moment to regroup, but it wasn't nearly long enough to make a difference. Rhys clung to his sheets, both overwhelmed but also superbly frustrated. This felt almost as good as the night before, but he felt an unfamiliar itch where he couldn't scratch, and he found himself rocking his pelvis along, unthinking.

Julian stopped for a brief laugh.

"Are you sure you don't want me to put something in here the way you're moving?"

Rhys blushed, mortified. Indeed, what the hell had he been doing just now? Was he more drunk than he'd realised?

"No…"

"No, you don't want me to, or no, you're not sure?"

"No… I'm not sure…" Rhys closed his eyes, ashamed. Wouldn't it have been so much easier, if… if he could have just been… since he enjoyed it so much, then he might as well have… He could have been, and then…

"Rhys." Julian's voice pulled him from his inner conflict. "You don't have to hate it. It's your body, whatever the shape, you're allowed to enjoy it."

"But—"

"This might sound crass, but I've done this to Quin countless times. I've probably stuffed every orifice he has, and they're much less pliable than yours. He's still a man, isn't he? There's no reason to worry about it if it's enjoyable for you. If you absolutely hate it, I'll stop, but you seem like you might want me to continue."

Might? His insides were tortured by the length of this speech. All he needed was a good enough excuse to not feel so rotten about it.

"F-fine..."

"I don't want you to feel like you're pressured to—"

"Just put the damn thing in there, I need to feel how it feels!" If it felt like shit, then that'd be the end of this.

"Aaa—!" How did it slide in there so effortlessly? Holy sh—

"It's in now."

"I don't need a fucking narrator! Sheesh— Aa, aah..."

After some tentative exploration, Julian withdrew his finger.

Rhys tried to catch his breath.

"Why did you stop?"

"If you're letting me put in my finger, couldn't you let the rest of me in there?"

Julian had seemed calm and collected all the way up to this point, but his expression neared the bothered childishness from dreamside.

"They're not the same size!" Rhys whispered with the maximum volume a whisper could have.

"It'll stretch..." He inserted a finger and pulled it gently sideways while giving it a twirl.

"Ahh." Rhys was surprised to realise it didn't hurt. He remembered it hurting a lot when he'd tried it before. Still, Julian's was of a worrisome size compared to his fingers.

"I'll be careful..." Julian crawled over Rhys and closer to his face, to a kissing distance. "I won't force it. It seems like it would fit. I don't mean to pressure you, but..." He looked miserable. Rhys reached for the front of his trousers to unclasp the button and confirm the source of his misery.

Maybe, Rhys found himself thinking. It might not be so bad.

"I'll let you," Rhys decided, "but only if..."

"Only if?"

"If you let me do the same to you dreamside." If Julian was serious about it not affecting the way he'd see Rhys, then for sure he wouldn't mind subjecting himself to the same treatment.

"Oh." Julian seemed to give it some thought. "Would that work? I suppose... that might work... I was able to do that stuff you instructed me to do."

Rhys had meant to make use of the back door like Julian had probably done with Quin, but apparently Julian's mind had taken it a step further.

"I'll do it. It might be interesting," Julian said with confidence.

"Really?"

"Yes, but unless you want to go do it right now, can we stop talking?" He leaned in to nuzzle against the side of Rhys's neck.

Somehow amidst all that, he'd managed to bare Rhys's lower half without Rhys realising.

He lowered himself to lay on top of Rhys, who was left with no doubts about the size and firmness of his cock. After receiving a permissive nod, he spread Rhys's legs apart carefully and positioned himself to where his fingers had been playing around a moment before.

"Relax. Remember to breathe," Julian whispered right by Rhys's ear.

Rhys had dreaded this moment most of his life, but when Julian let out a tiny contented grunt as he entered, something inside Rhys melted from the pleasure. He had no trouble letting the full length of it in.

"Hrr-hh a-a-ah."

What the hell was that? Was that coming from his own mouth? How? He hurried to shut himself up.

Julian pushed himself in, again.

The sound slipped out, again. It was no near-to-silent gasp like the ones before it.

Julian kissed Rhys's neck as he thrust himself in the third time. His grunts were soft and barely audible. Next to them, the strange sound coming out of Rhys's mouth was like an animal being strangled.

"Ahhnnggg, a-a-ah."

Oh no. There was no stopping it. Rhys tried to kiss Julian to keep himself from making noise, but it sounded even more lewd amidst the kisses.

If it hadn't felt this damn good, he might have had the self-control to stop, but with each thrust, he was already looking forward to the next.

A little more.

Maybe they were too busy to hear.

Just one more.

Maybe they were already asleep.

Oh God, that's the spot.

There was no way it would carry all the way over to the attic, right?

Ah, to hell with it.

All the way. In. There.

CHAPTER 3

A most unusual and intriguing sound reached Quin's ears as he sat in the lounge, reading a magazine and finishing his digestif.

It had been a single sound easily attributed to his ears playing tricks on him. As the silence resumed, he put it down to the sherry. Perhaps it was time to call it a night?

Just as he'd set the magazine aside, he heard it again. How sweet. It sounded rather like a baby goat but lighter and not as nasal.

Quin snorted from amusement, realising the who and the where and the likely reason for the noise, as the sporadic poorly stifled bleats grew lower and rougher in timbre.

Ah, that sounded like fun.

The decent thing would have been to retreat upstairs to let them have their privacy, but what harm would it do to stay? Wasn't it really on the two of them for having picked a location so easily overheard? They didn't seem to care and would likely remain none the wiser if Quin kept his mouth shut.

But he'd better have something at hand to make it seem like he wasn't merely eavesdropping if someone turned up, so he picked up his magazine again and turned his gaze back to the article he'd been reading.

Rhys had such a lovely voice. He was clearly still trying to restrain himself, but no matter Julian's memory loss, by the sounds of it, his wide catalogue of ways to make a person struggle with self-restraint seemed intact.

Ah, a nasty pang of jealousy made Quin seethe in the most disgustingly delicious manner as he pondered whose place in that room he would have rather taken. He set aside the magazine and breathed in slowly.

Rhys deserved to have this. In fact, Quin had been wishing for it. He just hadn't realised how conflicted he would feel having to listen to it.

The noise was getting really rather difficult to ignore, now. The walls did a poor job of muffling anything, so Quin could imagine most of what was going on based on personal experience and sounds alone.

It seemed an act of self-harm to remain here, so he stood up, but, instead of heading up to his room in the attic, he found himself inching closer to the door to Rhys's bedroom. This truly was considered poor form, wasn't it?

Quin leaned on the wall next to the door and closed his eyes, slightly grossed out by his own state. If it were anyone other than Rhys, he would have barged in there and joined the fun, but even warmed by the sherry, Quin was not foolish enough to disturb something this delicate and precious.

How awful would it be to stay here and let his hand wander into his breeches to relieve some of this tension, though? He was about to succumb to the urge when he was interrupted by Victor's rumbling whisper.

"Is he having a nightmare?"

Oh you sweet, innocent man! Quin found himself blushing and quickly moved his hands behind his back.

"No, it's fine. You should go back to your room," he whispered back in haste.

"What are they—?" Victor leaned closer to press his ear to the door as if the sounds from the room weren't clear enough to make out. They were loud enough to have alerted him from the attic, so surely he had a fairly good idea of what was causing them?

"We should give them some privacy." Quin was in dire need of some privacy himself. He felt light-headed. With each low groan coming from the bedroom, he could feel his insides frothing and his blood packing to his groin to the point it was becoming an inarguable discomfort.

Victor was looking at him, concerned. He seemed to be asking whether Quin was all right, but his usual difficulty with words had perhaps again kicked in.

"I'm fine." Quin swallowed. Shit, if it hadn't been so rude to use someone as a substitute, he could have—

Victor almost dropped his brush from the surprise. What was that? It had sounded like Rhys, but that had been no sound he'd heard Rhys ever make.

He hesitated only for a moment before heading down the stairs. Quin was already there but hadn't rushed into the bedroom.

"Is he having a nightmare?" It didn't sound anything like the nightmares before, but Victor was still a tad too alarmed to grasp what else it could be. Quin flinched.

"No, it's fine. You should go back to your room."

"What are they—?" Victor listened closer. He wasn't hugely experienced, but, with an ear pressed to the door, he could definitely tell what was happening on the other side.

"We should give them some privacy." Quin sounded out of sorts. Victor could empathise. He'd known this day would come eventually, and he was genuinely happy for Rhys, but he would have lied if he'd said it didn't also make him just a tiny bit sad.

Quin seemed to be taking it worse, though. Either that, or he was drunk, or having a seizure of some sort. Victor frowned.

"I'm fine."

"You don't look fine." Victor took a step closer in case the man was going to faint.

"I'm fine, I'm just... E-extremely horny."

Oh. Victor blinked. He'd never heard anyone be brazen enough to say something like that. He couldn't even fathom how someone could when he himself struggled with even the daily greetings.

Quin was fascinating.

Victor realised he was staring and looked away. As he looked away, his attention was drawn right back to the sounds coming from the bedroom. What was Julian doing in there to produce that from Rhys?

"What on earth are they doing..." he heard himself whisper, surprised he'd said it out loud, unthinking.

"I know exactly what they're doing." Quin leaned on the wall and closed his eyes. Was it painful to know, or was he busy imagining it? Victor couldn't decide whether to be envious.

Quin cracked an eye to look at Victor from under his subtly curved, extended eave of eyelashes. He could have formed a pagoda by stacking them on top of one another. No wonder he was having such trouble staying upright.

"Would you like to know?"

His voice was barely audible, but it wasn't because he'd wavered. He'd only lowered his volume to be discreet, to not disturb. His words hung in the air as if he'd shouted them from the top of his lungs, and they kept echoing within Victor's mind long after they had been drowned out by the sound of Rhys being pleasured to death.

How much would it cost to find out? It seemed safer not to know, and somehow Quin looked like he wasn't going to tell. This had sounded more like an offer for a demonstration.

That splendidly eaved eye was still looking straight at Victor, even if its owner seemed like he might collapse from a mere gust.

"I'm sorry, do I make you uncomfortable?" Quin finally turned away. "I'll go." He looked like he might fall over, so Victor quickly grabbed his hand. He turned to look, visibly confused. "What is it?"

If only there were a button to press or a lever to pull that would remove whatever kept the right words in, but alas, Victor was left silent with both his curiosity and concern.

It wasn't going to happen with Julian, but wouldn't this be the closest equivalent?

As soon as he'd thought the thought, he was appalled by its selfishness. No one deserved to be a stand-in to ease someone's heartbreak, and moreover, there was never going to be a substitute for Julian!

Victor was distracted by a squeal. He turned to face the door feeling almost *annoyed* by the interruption. What the hell were they doing in there?

"That's the best part..." Quin let out a heavy sigh and seemed to make a half-hearted effort to cool his flustered face with the back of his free hand.

Victor gritted his teeth. If he let go of Quin's hand, his time would be up. He would have wanted more time to consider it through and to prepare himself to say what he wanted to say. But there was never enough time, was there?

He leaned into it.

Quin was about to resign from any hope of enjoying the rest of the evening, even if that had meant on his own up in his room. It was getting too uncomfortable and too depressing, and no matter his libido, this state of arousal would not last forever. The last of the sherry had gone to his head with a pleasant, mild buzz, but that, too, would soon fade away as he'd only meant it as a digestif or an early nightcap.

This reminded him of the time at Agnes Point when he'd had to watch the two of them play together, with his wound on the side of his mouth still freshly stitched and delicate, barring him from participating. The scar seemed to ache from the memory, so he licked it before he realised it might be off-putting for Victor.

Quin glanced to see whether Victor had been looking and was startled by the man's face so close to his own.

There was no time to ask questions or analyse what this proximity might mean since a mouth was soon where his questions should have been, and someone else's tongue slid across the scar he'd only just licked.

He felt the back of his head hit the wall with a thunk, but he was already too rattled for it to make a difference, and if anything, it shook him out of his budding gloom.

"Can you be rougher?" he whispered as his breath quickened. It didn't seem in Victor's nature, but there was a promising hint of irritation in his eyes, and, after a pause as if to confirm, 'is this what you mean?', he bit Quin's lower lip.

What a precious Mountain Dog eager to serve!

Quin relaxed and let himself be pinned to the wall. In all honesty, he wasn't sure how he would have remained standing with his knees turning to jelly from Victor's surprisingly forceful kiss. This was not bad. This was not bad at all. There was almost no chance for him to even breathe!

"Ah, are you mad at me...?" he managed between kisses.

"No." This did not seem entirely truthful. Quin pulled him back by the hair at his neck.

"Really? Not even a little?"

"You're an annoying little shit, and I'm jealous. Is that what you wanted to hear?"

Quin gasped at the words coming out of that mouth.

"Yes." And more would be welcome, but he feared they were already making a fair amount of noise. The pair in the bedroom seemed too busy to hear, but Quin could still muster a morsel of consideration in case they were going to take a breather, so he refrained from begging.

Victor lifted him up on the wall much the same way as he'd done to Julian at Agnes Point, but instead of just holding him there, he also grabbed a hold of Quin's crotch. Quin tried hard to not let out a sound, but there was no way of holding this in.

"Ah, not so— Not— Don't—"

Why was he telling Victor to slow down when all he wanted to do was egg him on? At least his incompetent, bumbling mouth was sealed with another kiss.

"Don't bait me unless you're ready for the consequences." Victor tightened his grip.

"More..." Quin was ready to forget everything else. He felt himself be lifted again and pushed against the wall with a kiss, only this time the wall was not the wall, and it gave way unexpectedly.

"Aaah—!"

Victor fell on top of him. Rhys's startled face peeked over the side of the bed. Julian frowned behind him.

Quin had no time to panic when Victor pulled him up like a ragdoll and threw him over his shoulder.

"Apologies for the intrusion. I will fix the door tomorrow. Please carry on." He sounded surprisingly calm. When he turned around to leave, Quin was the one struggling with the words.

"Sorry!" was all he could think to yell as he was carried back out the door and to the stairs.

R hys's heart was pounding from the scare. He saw Victor carry Quin away, the door off its hinges on the floor and the open doorway into the empty hall. His hands were shaking, and he turned to stare at them instead. It felt as though he was about to pass out despite gasping for air.

His hands were clean. They were clean. He touched his face and his fingertips brushed upon something wet.

He wanted to hurl.

"Rhys?"

Rhys turned to look at Julian. Julian wrapped him into a tight embrace, triggering the sobs, but Julian also stroked the back of his head and held him tight until the sobs subsided.

It took Rhys a while to find his way back to the right time and place. His face wasn't covered in blood; it was just his tears. He dried them to the front of Julian's shirt and wailed tiredly.

"I'm sorry... I ruined it..."

It must have been incredibly frustrating to stop abruptly after all that, and Rhys was not sure how to get back to the previous mood after revisiting his trauma.

"It's fine. Don't worry about it. Was it the noise?" Julian confirmed.

Rhys nodded. With just that crash, he'd felt like he'd been yanked back to the attic laboratory, with the added horror of being naked, exposed and vulnerable. His body trembled.

"We're not in a hurry. It's thanks to you that I have all the time in the world." Julian hung the duvet over Rhys's shoulders, wrapped him in it and gave him a kiss. After the kiss, Rhys leaned on him, hoping to regain his calm. It gave him a moment to sit with his jumbled thoughts.

"Was it any good before we were interrupted?" He'd been too busy keeping everyone out, so it only now occurred to him that he might be lacking in this respect also. Julian's preferences had revolved around Quin before. Rhys's was conveniently self-lubricating, but did it feel any good if Julian was partial to something likely tighter and different? He had a butt, but that seemed even less like a hole he wanted anyone to fill.

"What the hell are you worried about now?" Julian ruffled Rhys's hair and smiled. His smiles were such a rare treat, Rhys felt instantly soothed by it.

No.

What was this feeling?

Was this what Quin felt when he made that disgusting, adoring melty face when he looked at Julian? A lot of things about Quin made no sense, but this seemed like it might. Rhys felt a strange, warm, fuzzy feeling when Julian smiled at him.

"It was very, very enjoyable, Rhys," Julian said in a low voice. He sounded like he was savouring the memory. "The real question is whether you liked it enough to let me do it again when you feel better."

Rhys thought about it and blushed. He didn't think he could get back into the mood, but his mind was suddenly revolving around the sensation of Julian inside of him. He slumped. Shit. Why did it feel like he was broken and twisted? He'd been appalled by the thought for so long, it seemed *wrong* and very much not allowed.

"We can think of something else to do if it wasn't to your liking. The important thing is that you enjoy yourself."

The important thing is—

Rhys closed his eyes. This was his chance to back out of it permanently. Julian seemed genuinely understanding.

"I enjoyed myself," Rhys whispered. In fact, now that he was past his scare, the distracting feeling he'd had all day was back but this time worse by about tenfold. He wanted something in there, deep enough to produce that pleasurable rush that ran through his whole body.

Rhys had spent most of his life in such unyielding denial, he'd never realised how many muscles and nerve-endings he had down there, and it now felt like he'd woken a tiny beast ready to burrow around within his insides.

"What is that face you're making? Do you want me to do something?" Julian cupped his cheek and looked him in the eye. Dammit, that smile. "You're going to have to tell me. This looks like you might want to resume, but I'm still not comfortable just assuming."

Rhys tried to make himself glare, but his brain was turning into mush. Why the hell was this man so bloody handsome? He'd definitely not been like this a year ago!

Rhys pounced on Julian to kiss him and to sit on top of him. The binder had long since fallen off, so Julian's hands caught him, touching bare skin. Rhys thwarted his surprised gasp by kissing the man.

"Your body is beautiful, imperfections and all." Julian ran his fingers over the shapes and the scars that had caused Rhys immeasurable heartache, but his smile seemed to wipe all of it away like it no longer mattered. "This scrawny sack of flesh and scarred skin is giving me everything that's housed inside that head of yours. Please take good care of it for me. Please use it to enjoy yourself in any way you can. You deserve to feel at home in your body, regardless of how it has let you down."

Rhys tried to concentrate on the words, but the sound of Julian's voice was massaging his heated insides, proving almost as distracting as the hands against his skin and the hard cock under him.

"Tell me later." Rhys adjusted his seat until he could feel that hard-on settle in a spot in the middle, where it instinctively felt good as he rubbed himself against it. Blood coursed through him, the pleasure making him feel weak in the knees. "Ah." How embarrassing that his body would do this just from feeling Julian against him.

"Does it feel good like this?" Julian looked surprised.

Rhys was too out of breath to reply but forced himself to nod. He had no idea how any of it worked, but there was something there, under his skin, throbbing and making him want to rub it.

Julian reached down there with a hand to feel the source of Rhys's novel obsession.

"Aah... Aa... haah... Not— so hard— it's—" Rhys lifted himself up and out of reach. "Ahh, sensitive."

"Rhys."

"Hmmmh?"

"I think it's your penis."

"Huh?" Rhys tried to understand those words. Had he fallen asleep at some point? He looked down there but saw nothing but hair.

"Here." Julian brought his hand up to it and nudged it gently.

"Ah..." There was something there but it was hardly big enough to be called anything.

"I bet it's bigger. I think it's just not all the way out."

Rhys let out a nervous chuckle and swallowed. Intense relief washed over him before he could even fully understand the words, and along with it, his tears wet his cheeks.

"It's all there, though, as far as I'm concerned." Julian dried some of the tears with his thumb. "Whoever claims anything different is a blind fool."

Rhys burst out laughing and kissed him. The stupid man! Why was he this bloody irresistible? He could get away with saying the stupidest things with that face of his. Rhys wiped off the rest of his tears. "Shut up, and fuck me silly."

Victor let Quin down at the top of the stairs, but because he looked ready to fall over, Victor lifted him back up and sat him down on his bed instead.

"Uh?" The man frowned perplexed. "What about the rest of it...?"

Truth be told, Victor had been hoping to go with the flow and get through this with sheer determination, but ever since the Eve and seeing Quin, Julian and Rhys so badly banged up, he'd had trouble adjusting to the fragile nature of the human body.

He was not back to feeling like himself, either, even if his thigh had healed remarkably well. It probably wasn't smart for him to be carrying anyone up the stairs just yet, but thankfully the wound felt like it would hold, it didn't hurt too bad, and he no longer felt as sickeningly faint and dizzy as on the days following the blood loss.

But Quin.

Victor sighed and knelt in front of him.

"Does it hurt?"

"What?"

"Your ribs. I fell on top of you." He patted through Quin's sides carefully to test whether they seemed sore and to bring them to Quin's attention since the man could have stood to be a little more aware of his own condition.

Quin winced.

"It's nothing. Let's continue."

Victor added the smallest amount of pressure, and, as expected, made Quin yelp. Quin looked up at him, face aggrieved by disbelief and disappointment.

"You're not saying that was it?" He sounded only inches away from being reduced to a whine.

"You like it rough, don't you?" There was no way to respond to his requests without potentially worsening his injuries.

"Oh, yes." His expression softened. "Don't worry about it and just do it. That's what Julian does..." He leaned back and closed his eyes.

"I'm not Julian, though."

"I know. I'm sorry." Quin sighed. He reopened his eyes and after a pause, added, "I can't think straight when I'm this pent up. Are you sure you're not up for it? I'll moan about the ribs later. They really don't hurt that bad."

"That's probably the sherry." It was Victor's turn to sigh. He sat on the bed next to Quin but with his back against the wall.

"You're too considerate. I'm not that frail."

Victor watched his delicate features, the ridiculously thick eyelashes, the teardrop-shaped dainty earring on his left ear and his fine, wavy hair that had escaped the hair tie during their scuffles. None of it roused particular confidence in his ability to withstand anything but the gentlest of treatments, even if he'd shown considerable resilience in the face of Mr Murray, and presumably would have had to put up with a much rougher version of Julian during their past relationship.

Ah, this is going to require some resilience from me, too, Victor thought. He could feel the dread building in the pit of his stomach. Casual topics were no problem. He was fairly used to Quin, and the man was inexplicably easy to talk to under most circumstances. But getting this said would require some extra mustering of courage.

"It's not just your ribs I'm worried about."

"Oh?"

Victor watched the wall opposite and breathed steadily.

"I want to help you. I just don't know how." He closed his eyes. It wasn't as if a little embarrassment would hurt, but the acid burning a hole through his stomach, regardless, did.

Quin said nothing, so Victor checked whether he'd perhaps fallen asleep, tired of waiting. He was watching back, face neutral.

"Don't look at me like that. I'm not altogether inexperienced. I've just never been with another man." There. That part of it was out.

"I can teach you. It's not that difficult. I'll show you what Julian likes if you want some practice." Quin seemed to cheer up. He turned on his side to face Victor.

"Ah, no, that's all right. I'd rather Julian tell me himself if he wants to." Victor blushed. It was likely never going to happen, but he liked to think it might.

"Fair."

"But if you want me to do something…"

"Oh, I know! How about you show me how you usually do it to yourself? That could be interesting." Quin's eyes lit up.

"You'll be disappointed."

"I've been jerking myself off for a damn decade. I could go for a change of pace."

Victor raised an eyebrow. Quin had the air of a person very willing to engage in these things with anyone or anything that moved. His relative abstinence shouldn't have come as a surprise considering how obsessed with Julian he was, yet it seemed unexpected that he'd been saving himself for so long.

"What?" Quin paused to think. "Well, more than a decade, but who's counting? Will you do it or not? You're not going to crack my ribs with a handjob, right?"

Victor let out a low laugh.

"True." It wasn't much of a request. "As long as you keep your expectations low and don't blame me if it's not up to your standards." He must have been desperate to make do with just a handjob.

"Where do you want me?"

"Stay there if you're comfortable."

J.B. THWAITE

V ictor sat closer to the edge of the bed, opened the front of Quin's robe and lowered his breeches.

Judging by his face, he'd probably expected all of this lengthy interlude to have softened Quin's dick, but it bounced up to greet him like a fresh, young willow switch.

The man tried to position his hand but, after a few tries, pulled Quin up to sit and took a seat behind him. Quin leaned back and made himself comfortable. Victor took a hold of the shaft and seemed to gauge it in his hand, to find the right grip. His hand felt nice and warm, a little rough but not as rough as Quin had expected.

Quin hummed contentedly. It wasn't what he'd had in mind for the evening, but anything other than his own boring hand was a plus. He'd experimented with oils and rags and all sorts of desperate measures to find a more desirable feel, but it was always going to be predictable, and he would always default back to his old ways just to get it over with.

"Oh, uh, huh?" His thoughts were interrupted by Victor's fingers brushing on his nipple. He'd tried to play with them on occasion with not a whole lot of success due to the predictability aspect. It had felt silly to even try. Julian's tongue was the only thing that made them perk up.

"Ahh..." It was doing something. What a pleasant surprise! "Ah... That's nice—ah, nice."

With just the barely audible, muffled sounds coming from downstairs, Quin's voice sounded crisp and clear, and it was soon making him feel self-conscious.

"Ah... ah... ah... ah..." Had he always sounded like this? Why? He tried to tone it down.

He'd managed near silence when Rhys had been doing this, and that had felt magical. This was just a matter-of-fact everyday handjob. Victor had prefaced it as nothing special.

"Hgn... Hh... hnn... Aah—!"

Something this steady should have been as boring and as predictable as if he'd done it himself, but what an oddly pleasurable pace. Quin didn't have the patience for something this leisurely. Even when he'd tried to take his time to savour it, he'd eventually always given in and defaulted to something quicker.

"Ah... ahh... ahhh..." Was it his imagination or was there an echo in here? He closed his eyes.

"Ohhh..." Even slower?! "Aahhhhh... I can't..."

Victor was doing something with his fingers that had no business feeling this good. They were sliding from the precum, and gently rubbing and tugging around the corona. There was very little give in his grip unless he loosened his hold, so when he pulled along the length of the shaft, it felt blissfully tight and commanding.

"Ahhh, aaahhh, aaahhh—!" Quin blushed from deep embarrassment. He was a complete idiot, so full of himself! He'd said he'd teach Victor!

He looked up to see Victor's face. The man looked concentrated but calm. Perhaps the beard played some part in it—at least Quin hoped so—because the expression remained unchanged while Victor played with Quin's nipple as if casually tuning an instrument. Having been reduced to this moaning, groaning and wailing bagpipe, it was hurting Quin's pride to see Victor so unaffected. It made him want to do a few select things to make the man make at least equal noise.

"What is it?"

"Ahhh... Aahh..."

"You don't like it?"

"Ahhnngh... Haah..." It wasn't until Victor paused that Quin could find his words. "What the hell is wrong with you?!"

"Sorry?"

"Liar! You were totally pulling wool over my eyes! Haah..."

Victor didn't even defend himself. He just watched Quin like an innocent little sheep. When Quin was about to further berate him for it, he opened his mouth.

"Did you want me to go on, or was it unsatisfactory?"

"Damn you, Victor!" Quin would have been angrier if his dick wasn't still throbbing in Victor's grip. The man was watching him, not admitting to anything. "Yes! Yes, I want you to continue. In fact, can you come into my room every night for some of this?" As he said it, Victor resumed what he'd been doing.

"I think you're just preconditioned to enjoy anything that's unfamiliar to you."

"Aah, hah, ah..." Quin tried to glare at him for making such polite conversation whilst playing him like a damn harp, but the pace was finally picking up and it was hitting a sweet spot.

When it did, Quin's mind was relieved of all thought. His body responded on its own accord, spasming pleasurably until he'd spilt everything he had, and the nagging horniness was replaced by a deep sense of satisfaction.

The only thing withdrawing from perfection was Victor's unearthly calm.

The man could have at least pretended to be a little affected by this!

"There's a clean handkerchief on my nightstand, if you'd like to—"

This time Quin managed a proper glare.

"What?" Victor looked startled.

"You really are completely partial to Julian, aren't you?"

"What?" Victor frowned.

"Doesn't this make you feel anything?"

Victor's frown deepened.

"Well?" Quin couldn't curb his impatience.

"I don't understand what you mean."

"Well, you—" Quin propped himself up somewhat to bring attention to the cause of his annoyance. "Huh?"

"I don't know what you were expecting, but that's not my thigh."

Quin opened his mouth, but this time he was thoroughly stumped.

There was a moment of excited dread where he wasn't sure whether he'd just missed out on something or dodged a bullet. He'd had a feeling it was hefty, but he hadn't expected it to grow to this size.

"Do you want me to return the favour?" Quin asked, unsure how to even go about it.

"It's fine, I get it..." Victor looked away.

"No, don't worry about it, I'll make it work. I can do it! I love challenges!" Quin braced himself.

"I can teach you," Victor said.

Quin stared at him.

It was partly obscured by his beard, but a sly smile appeared on Victor's lips.

Quin stared.

The room was silent save for the still-ongoing concert of moans coming from downstairs.

Quin recovered from his shock and started to laugh. Victor joined in with a chuckle.

"All right. I'd like that." Quin smiled back.

CHAPTER 5

A urora was holding in her excitement with the desperation of a sailor trying to stop a cannonball-sized leak with a sock and scooping water out of the ship with a broken sieve.

The cottage was perfect, just as she'd imagined. A path of stepping stones meandered through the yard past the cutest little tree—possibly Johan or Kurt—and a few mossy boulders, a bench and a little table. The door the steps led to had been painted bright blue, and there was a little hatch, which Sir Swifty promptly used so he didn't have to wait to be let in.

Ren led Jasmine by the hand. She dropped a few of the letters she was carrying on her way to the front door, so Aurora picked them up as she followed the girls.

"You can leave your shoes over there, and there are pegs for your coats here. Sorry it's so empty. We haven't lived here for very long." Ren kicked off her shoes and started to fuss, putting out some water and food for the cat and making a fire in a stove in the inglenook.

Vincent came in through what seemed to be the garage. Aurora caught a glimpse of a rightful mess in there but hid her amusement.

"Are you hungry? I could make us something." Vincent was caught in a similar energetic fussing as Ren.

Aurora winked at Jasmine, who looked puzzled by the nervous energy. The girl was a little more reserved than Ren and didn't talk much, but she'd mentioned this was her first time travelling apart from her family this far up north. She'd seemed excited to come, but this was no doubt also unnerving for her.

"Meatballs?" Ren asked, eyes glistening. "I'll air out the bedding and show Jasmine around while you're cooking." She practically ran down the short corridor to what were likely the bedrooms, with Jasmine following her like a graceful but confused lamb.

"Do you need help?" Aurora took off her shoes and walked over to Vincent who was carrying in their provisions.

"No, ah, I'm used to doing this myself..." He hauled a crate of food into the pantry. "You can make yourself comfortable in the meanwhile."

This left Aurora with idle hands in an unfamiliar environment. She wondered whether to sit down and wait, but it felt wrong not to help. But if she was only going to get in his way...? She frowned.

Vincent glanced at her.

"Well, you could help." Vincent scratched the back of his head. "But you could also go through the files Rhys had copied for you. I know you've been itching to get to them."

She'd felt awfully guilty asking to bring them along, but there was a big box full of files from Hosta, all to do with Vincent's brothers, with a number of connective failures she was keen to read about. Even now that Vincent's sleep had improved and he wasn't in such a dire need of help with it, Aurora was as determined as ever to find out the root cause of these issues.

The amount of data lost in the fire of the ReM Clinic was disconcertingly staggering, but she and Hosta had managed to recover some that they'd used as a nest egg to build upon. There was so much fascinating information out there now that Aurora knew where and what to look for. So many people whose lives wozuld benefit from it.

"You don't mind?"

"Of course not. My study is the first door on the right. There's a more comfortable chair in there. I can carry in your files if you'd like." He headed into the garage without waiting for an affirmative.

Yes. Very useful. The box was not light. He carried it like a champ. She followed him to the study and watched him set it on the desk, open the small window for some fresh air and make sure there was space on the desk and a pen and some paper for Aurora to use.

She drew closer to him instinctively, and when she blocked his way and their eyes met, he obliged her with a kiss.

He was always such a gentleman, treating her like a delicate flower, considerate to a flaw, yet when he kissed her now, she felt herself be pushed back until she almost fell over. He grabbed a hold of her and barely restrained himself from kissing her again.

"I need to—" He drew a deep breath. "Pardon me. I should go."

Vincent hurried out of the room, leaving Aurora to lean against the wall, confused and catching her breath.

Ah, he could have stayed a little while longer! Even if Ren and Jasmine were close by, a few kisses would have hardly made enough noise to disturb anyone.

Aurora peeked out of the room, watched Vincent get to cooking in the kitchen and pushed the door shut.

Useful for carrying heavy items, and troublesome in all the other ways.

It took her a moment to clear her head to be able to redirect her focus to her data.

Vincent drove them into town the following morning. He dropped the girls off a few streets earlier to pop into the local café for a decadent breakfast tea with some of the local baked delicacies.

"Take your time but don't be all too long, or Celandine will be mighty cross with me. You know how she feels about sweets as breakfast." Vincent handed Ren some money and helped her down from the cockpit recess.

"I know, I know. I'll tell her we had nothing but sandwiches with lettuce. You don't have to help me down. I can manage." Ren patted his hand and climbed down on her own the rest of the way.

Aurora was admittedly nervous enough to want to join the girls, but it would only delay the inevitable. With Ren and Jasmine out of earshot, she climbed up into the cockpit recess to take the place in front of Vincent.

"Do you think they'll like me? What if they hate me?"

Ren had mentioned the rest of their family so many times, Aurora had a fairly clear idea of what to expect, and, frankly, each time Aunt Celandine was mentioned, it made her stomach roil. She seemed an exacting and strict woman and important to both Ren and Vincent. If Aurora couldn't win her over, it would spell serious trouble for this relationship.

"Who could ever hate you?" Vincent looked pained. He took the controls but had some trouble reaching with Aurora there in between. Good thing he had such long arms.

Freya hovered leisurely the rest of the way and came to a stop next to the front door of a townhouse. Vincent set the speeder to her cool-down configuration.

Aurora hesitated, knowing he was waiting for her to get off.

"Are you sure they'll like me?" she couldn't resist asking.

"They'll love you. And even if they won't, they'll just have to live with it, because I'm not going to change my mind." He moved a stray lock of her hair behind her ear, but just as she thought he might kiss her and make this a sweet and intimate moment, he lifted her up from the seat and helped her over the side.

Not only was Aurora a cluster of nerves, but she also found herself perplexed by his brisk behaviour.

"Let's not keep them waiting, though. I'm sure they're eager to meet you." Vincent jumped down to the sidecar and swooped her along with him. He held her securely until she was firmly on the ground, but his haste left her startled.

Vincent knocked on the door, opened it and announced their arrival.

"Vincent?! Is that you?" A woman's face appeared from what seemed to be the kitchen. "Celandine is baking. She'll be done in a bit. Vincent?"

"Yes, it's me—"

"Who is this?" She raised her brows and eyed Aurora sharply.

"Aurora Vesper, nice to meet you." Aurora offered her a trembling hand, hoping its tremble wasn't as obvious as it felt.

"Oh, you're Dr Vesper? My name is Aster Bramble. Pleased to make your acquaintance, and thank you for treating our Vincent. Has he been giving you trouble? Why has he dragged you all the way out here?" She took Aurora's hand for a brief shake and continued to eye her, expecting answers.

Aurora opened her mouth but couldn't decide what to answer first or how.

"Is George at home? I would like him to be here as well," Vincent interrupted and climbed a few steps up the stairs in the front hall, presumably to look.

Another woman, this time likely the infamous Celandine, appeared from the kitchen with her hands and arms caked in flour. She raised her brow similarly to her sister, but it made her look significantly more frightening considering her size, stature and the rest of her expression.

"Who is this?" she repeated Mrs Bramble's question, sounding like she'd caught an intruder in her house. "Where is Ren? You're not letting her run around town by herself first thing in the morning, are you?"

Aurora felt compelled to defend herself as if she'd made the decision to let the girls enjoy their tea.

"This is Dr Vesper. The doctor that's been helping Vincent with... sleep issues, was it?" Mrs Bramble explained.

"Yes, a pleasure to meet you." Aurora offered her hand.

Celandine looked at it, her expression tightening, and lifted her hands as if to explain to a fool she wasn't going to partake in handshakes in the middle of her baking.

Was this really going to be OK? Didn't she rather seem like she might hate her already?

"A woman doctor? That is commendable. Superfluous, but commendable." Celandine huffed. "Wouldn't a nurse have been fine enough? Well, I suppose it's not all bad to be ambitious. Must be keeping you busy all day. Does Mr Vesper make enough money to afford a housekeeper?"

Well, that expelled that doubt, Aurora thought. The woman clearly despised her.

"There is no Mr Vesper other than my father, but I can manage on my own. Thank you for your concern." Aurora made a spirited effort to smile.

"George! Vincent is here," Mrs Bramble yelled up the stairs. "He will be right down. I swear, he's getting slower by the year."

"We're not in a hurry," Vincent said.

Aurora wished they had been in a hurry.

An awkward silence descended until Mr Bramble appeared at the top of the stairs and started his way down.

"Where is Ren?" the man asked once he'd determined with some apparent difficulty that there were no children present.

"She's having breakfast tea at the café with my sister Jasmine. I'll introduce you later." Vincent gave Mr Bramble a hug.

"Sister?"

"Yes, I rang and told you about it after Midwinter, remember?"

"Ah, Aster mentioned something. Who is this lovely lady?" Mr Bramble took Aurora's hand into both of his and kissed it like a gentleman.

"This is Aurora," Vincent introduced her to him.

Mr Bramble mulled it only briefly, smiled at Aurora and turned to Vincent.

"You're in love with her? Is she the one?"

"Yes."

Aurora felt herself turn red to the very core from feeling abashed and warmed by the sentiment. It seemed more impactful when he was admitting it to someone else so openly.

The sisters appeared to have been less astute than the close-to-blind Mr Bramble and were now choking on air and spit. Mrs Bramble recovered from her shock more quickly, and before Aurora could fully understand what was happening, she had been engulfed into a hug.

"Is this true? Is it mutual?" Mrs Bramble seemed excited.

Aurora nodded and was squeezed into a hug once more.

"Finally! I was so worried he would be left all on his own." Mrs Bramble measured Aurora from head to toe. "See. What did I tell you, sister?"

"Yes, you did say he would find someone." Celandine sighed and, to set up the thinnest, most useless veil of privacy, pulled her sister a few steps aside where their conversation was still fully audible. "Will someone so ambitious and career-oriented provide much companionship, though? Will she have time for anything other than her own interests? Such a highly educated woman must be difficult to converse with. And what of Ren? Isn't she nearing a delicate age where she could use some steady motherly guidance?"

"I understand your concerns, but," Mrs Bramble lowered her voice further, "he is not getting any younger. Perhaps she will hear reason—"

"Pray tell, what sort of reason are you suggesting I hear?" Aurora stifled her annoyance and forced herself to keep smiling.

"We can discuss it later, luv. You must be tired from your trip. Would you like some breakfast? Coffee? Tea? How long will you be staying?" Mrs Bramble deflected with her questions.

Aurora felt Vincent take her hand. It was warm and comforting.

"There is no need for you to pester her with the sort of discussion you're thinking of." Vincent's voice wavered none despite Celandine glaring at him. She was about to object when Vincent continued, "I appreciate your concern, but frankly in this instance, you can stuff it."

Aurora blinked. Was he deliberately trying to start a fight over this?

Celandine opened her mouth but was cut short again.

"No, Celandine. You're just going to have to trust my judgement."

"Vincent—"

"If I find out you've accosted her with your inane ideas against my wishes, I will not forgive you. I won't repeat myself."

"That's fine, luv." Mrs Bramble patted his arm. "I'll have a talk with my sister later."

"No need." Celandine excused herself and returned to the kitchen.

Aurora glanced at Vincent, worried. She did not want to become a source of strife between him and his family. She wondered what sort of concessions she'd have to make to get on Celandine's good side. It might be difficult to meet the woman's expectations without compromising her career as a doctor and a scientist.

Vincent squeezed her hand and smiled at her reassuringly.

"How about it? Would you like some tea or coffee?" He turned back to Mrs Bramble. "I purposely skipped breakfast this morning. I've missed her breakfast rolls. Would you make us some tea?"

Mrs Bramble smiled and gave him a good, long hug, and the tension from before was more or less gone. Then she took him and Aurora by the hand and pulled them along into the kitchen for some breakfast.

R en and Jasmine arrived an hour later, and the questions dealt to Aurora were directed towards Jasmine instead. Aurora felt bad for her but was glad for the breather. She slipped away from the dining table, to her mind without anyone noticing, but Vincent followed her only a half a minute later.

"Are you all right?" He led her aside into a sitting room across the hall.

"Yes. I just wanted a moment to myself," Aurora explained hastily.

"Ah, should I leave you to it?"

How are you being so considerate yet so dense at the same time? Do you not want to spend a moment with me?

"I'm sorry." Vincent towered in front of her, looking down like a Learian deerhound caught doing something naughty.

Aurora tested his forehead out of habit, but it felt normal. Was his connection still misfiring? What other conditions were there that made him tune in like that?

"I'm not sure. I think I can do it much the same way as when I fall asleep nowadays: by concentrating. I instinctively did something to tune it out before, and then realised I could reverse it just the same." Vincent had developed a habit of rearranging locks of her hair when he seemed nervous. "Sometimes it happens on its own without me realising. Are you upset with me? I'll try not to if it bothers you."

"It is a little unsettling..." Not that she had all that many secrets that she wanted to keep hidden, but she was concerned that having him hear all of the embarrassing little things that popped into her head might make him think less of her—

"I wish that were true. I sometimes think so much of you, it's excruciating." Vincent's fingers lingered at the few loose strands of hair at her temples. "Also, I'm not entirely sure what you meant with dense just now. It's a fair judgement for sure, but I think you were referring to something more specific. Did I miss something important?"

"You just seemed so eager to leave..."

"I said I wouldn't go unless you wanted me to. I just wanted to make sure."

"Stay." Aurora fingered the front of his shirt.

Was it really that easy? All she needed to do was command him, like a dog?

"Yes. That's how easy it is. Exactly like a dog. I'll be your dog." Vincent wrapped his arms around her and rested his chin on top of her head.

"A little too tall for a dog." Aurora pressed her cheek on his chest.

"I'll grovel on my hands and knees for you if that's what you want."

Don't do that, silly. You'll hurt your back.

Tall people were already more likely to have back problems, and besides, would he even be able to with his knee the way it was? Not to mention the shoulder.

"I might not be at my best, but I can still grovel for you, at least." Vincent grinned. "I may have to pull you down to the floor with me, though, if I can't get up."

"Let's not do that on the floor. We do have beds—" It wasn't until she'd said it out loud that she realised how suggestive it sounded. She blushed.

"I wish I could in good conscience carry you upstairs to one right now." Vincent's hold of her waist tightened.

"Save the athletics for later. I can walk up there myself."

Alas, whatever was up there was not on the cards as Ren knocked on the sitting room door at that most unfortunate moment.

"Aunt Aster was asking where the two of you went. Should I tell her you're in here, fastened to each other by the hip?" she asked.

Aurora wondered if it were possible to blush both inside and out.

"Keep the details to yourself, and I'll promise to be understanding when you're of the age to find somebody for yourself," Vincent responded to the girl. To Aurora he whispered to add, "at the ripe age of at least thirty-five."

"What? You want her to become a spinster?" Aurora whispered back.

"A doctor or a mechanic will do as well but something she can support herself with."

"I'll tell her you're coming in a moment," Ren called from the other side of the door, "but you know she'll be in here in a heartbeat if she realises you might be up to something indecent."

"We are merely having a conversation, Ren. We will be right there." Vincent lowered his voice once more, this time considerably more perturbed, "How does she even know anything about anything indecent? Who has she been talking to about such things?"

"She's probably just overheard it and doesn't know what it means." Aurora looked up at him. He bowed down closer.

"You'll have to excuse me, but I'm not the brightest of dogs. Could you show me what it means?"

Aurora gave him a pointed look.

"You know this is not the place." Too many people to walk in on a demonstration of something indecent.

Vincent looked dejected.

"Where and when would that be, then?" He seemed to have realised how slim their chances were for privacy without outright asking for some, consequently opening the conversation for speculations.

They might have a better chance back at the cottage, but the girls would have to come up with something to do outside for long enough to avoid the risk of getting caught. Alternatively, they would have to do it silently when the girls were asleep, and there was no getting around the risk of either of them waking up and walking in on them.

"Might not be for a while." Aurora patted his cheek. He seemed to want to bite her fingers but nuzzled against them instead. The dog knew some self-restraint. She smiled.

"I will do my best." Vincent closed his eyes, looking tortured.

"You'll get your treat. You just need to wait for it for a while longer."

CHAPTER 6

Rhys watched Julian tap the pharmacy counter, face rigid but with the general air of a bear shot in the arse, about to explode. He'd had some issues with the last few clients, and he'd been in a mood since he'd woken up this morning. His civility was attached to the rest of him by a thread as thin as spider's web, and one errant pull seemed like it might be the difference between his usual bearable customer service and a full-on verbal beating.

Quin came in through the back door, sweaty from a jog. Rhys had been feeling unwell, so he'd declined the offer to join. The weather was drizzly but not cold, yet it didn't seem smart to tempt fate.

"Is he done soon?" Quin wiped his face on a towel he had draped over his shoulder.

"The pharmacy will be open for another half an hour, but I'm hoping this is the last customer."

"Is it as bad as after lunch?"

"I tried to get him to relax by helping him out for a moment, but he insists it's fine. I think I may have made it worse by making him feel like I'm breathing down his neck."

"Do you want me to give it a try?"

At this point, a controlled explosion seemed better than letting Julian reach a boiling point on his own, but Rhys couldn't in good conscience send someone knowingly in harm's way.

Then again, this was Quin.

"Would you? What am I saying, of course you would."

Quin shuddered, chuckled and scratched the back of his neck. He peeked into the pharmacy to determine the extent of the problem and licked his lips in his usual half-nervous half-excited manner.

"It looks bad."

"Doesn't it?" Rhys sighed. He'd had a feeling it was worse than normal.

"Yeah, I might not survive, unless..." There was a hint of a grin that he tried to disguise by tapping the side of his mouth with a finger. "Do you mind, if I—?"

"Use whatever means you deem necessary."

Julian's temper seemed stretched enough to not be resolved with a good night's sleep, so an intervention now would probably yield better results than waiting for it to pass.

"Don't worry. I'll return him to you disarmed and in working order. Go and get some rest so your cold doesn't get worse." Quin patted Rhys on the back.

"Try not to break anything, all right? That includes yourself. Don't get too carried away."

"You can stay and watch if you're worried." Quin gave him his usual roguish grin and, having received his permission, did not stay to hear further comments.

Rhys sat down on a step out of sight with no intention of forming a solitary audience, but with Julian in such a sour mood, it would have been irresponsible of him not to stay for a few minutes to make sure the two of them weren't about to kill each other with their foreplay.

Julian was glad to be rid of the latest customer. It was rarely this bad even when some of them tested his patience, but Rhys seemed to be coming down with something and hadn't slept very well the previous night. He'd refused any medicine, saying it wasn't needed, and Julian had stayed up half the night with a nagging feeling he should have done something.

Part of it may have been that he'd been looking forward to some stress relief after a hectic week, but Rhys had needed to rest, so even a casual encounter dreamside had been out of the question.

Julian was looking forward to going upstairs for a snack and a nightcap and to retire in his room to wind down in silence. He just needed to finish rolling the last batch of pills and lock the front door a half an hour from now.

The minutes seemed to be ticking away at a snail's pace, but the snail had long since succumbed to the blasting midday sun and become a sticky blob of inanimate goo.

"Bloody fuck-knuckle!" Some of the pills rolled off the grooved pill tray when he flinched, not expecting Quin to turn up. "Can you not skulk around like a damn thief?"

Quin's presence had been gradually getting less tiresome, even almost bearable, but the deep irritation was back today and spared no hostages.

"I can, and I wasn't. What are you making?"

"Not today, Quin."

"Rhys said it was fine." Quin flashed him what was quite frankly an illegal smirk.

"Rhys? Did you disturb him when he's supposed to rest?" Julian crouched down to collect the pills he'd dropped to dispose of them. "What is that smell?"

"I went out for a run." Quin was still smiling, looking smug. "I know you like it."

What in the name of the bloody Guardian was this supposed to be? A deliberate effort to get him to lose his shit?

"Did Rhys say something to you?" The boy had promised not to spread the things Julian had blabbed about whilst uninhibited dreamside. Surely, he wouldn't—

Quin leaned closer to keep his voice down.

"Why do you think I'm always in such good shape?" His clothes looked moist and cool from the rain, but he seemed to have made some effort to wipe himself dry judging by the towel on his shoulder and his cheek emanating warmth so close to Julian's ear. There was no escaping the smell of sweat.

"Disgusting." Julian brushed him off.

"Liar." Quin smacked him with his towel.

"What the hell do you think you're doing?! I'm trying to work!" About to completely lose it, Julian grabbed the front of Quin's shirt but remembered in the nick of time that he was supposed to keep quiet to not disturb Rhys in case the boy was sleeping. "Stop riling me up. This is hard enough as it is." He turned back to rolling his pills.

"Are these sugar pills?" Quin snatched one and popped it into his mouth.

"For the ever-loving Guardian, Quin! Are you a complete imbecile? Spit that out at once!"

"Come and get it." The man propped the pill between his teeth.

"That's a damn laxative, you ass!" This got him to spit it out and toss it in the bin.

"Well, don't you have anything nicer for me to try?" The damn nincompoop fingered some of the pill bottles on the counter.

"Get your paws off of the laudanum this instant, or I swear I'll throw you out of here!"

"You're really no fun." He popped another one of the supposed laxatives to call Julian's bluff. All Julian could do was try to shake off the worsening irritation.

"Don't blame me if you get the runs. Idiot."

He wished he'd made this batch stronger than usual to teach Quin a lesson, but unfortunately, these were the type of pills his customers took for every little ailment to keep them from seeking out the more harmful remedies. To avoid overdose, they could only contain the bare minimum of anything that would make a difference.

"Hmm, tastes like saffron, ginger... Rhubarb maybe?" Quin seemed to be taking his time, rolling the pill around in his mouth. After watching him at it for a while, Julian came back to his senses.

"I've had it with your crap. From now on, stay out of my pharmacy when I'm working, or I'll—!"

"You'll what?" Quin made no move to comply, and his feet seemed glued to the floorboards. When Julian tried to shove him away, he bounced right back, unaffected. "You keep threatening me, but you're all bark and no bite."

"May I remind you who gave you this." Julian squeezed Quin's cheeks to get him to open his mouth for a full view of the scar. Out of a moment's impulse, he stretched that side of Quin's mouth until the man finally stopped grinning and looked pained.

"You did." Quin's grin did not return when Julian let go, but he had that same expression on his face as he'd had just before he'd received the scar.

There was no drink to muddle the senses, but much as Julian had guessed, the mere sight of him was as intoxicating. Ever since Midwinter Eve, the effect was compounded by a feeling of inexplicable familiarity, like Quin was no longer just a stranger he'd met no more than a year ago. The intensity was still unnerving, but it seemed to make more intuitive sense.

Julian grabbed a hold of Quin's throat and held him still, fighting the urge to take the bait.

It was easier to resist when he knew to expect it, but he was tired from having to restrain himself and hence undeniably tempted.

Quin was starting to look like he might lose his consciousness, so Julian eased his hold. The man looked back at him with the most bleary, loving eyes, as if he'd also lost all of his senses.

"What is wrong with you?" This confusion did help Julian regain some feeble self-control, but the uncomfortable urge to do that again was as pressing as ever.

"You." Quin's mouth melted into a happy smile. "You're what's wrong with me. Please be wrong with me again."

Julian's mind went blank. He was ravenous. He wanted to devour all of Quin but started with the mouth still tasting of saffron and ginger. The smell of sweat he'd deemed so disgusting only moments prior was now arousing him further.

Quin bent backwards across the counter, toppling a few bottles and boxes in the process.

"Do it. Please. I need this." He groped at the front of Julian's shirt and forced himself in, popping a few buttons in the process. His hands were cool from his run outside but felt pleasant against Julian's heated skin. They gravitated into an embrace like two puzzle pieces fitting together.

"Ah, shit." Julian tried to regain his senses and back off. "Rhys..." This was not right. Not without at least asking! Had he meant what he'd said before, or...?

Quin pulled him back and sought his eyes.

"I told you. He said it was fine. I promise you, it's fine. You can flog me and throw me out if I'm wrong."

Was this good enough? Could he really? If he couldn't do and have all of everything, then at least another kiss... one or two more tastes of this. Just a little bit more...

"Ahhhh, Jules..." Quin hung heavily on his neck and tried to catch his breath.

"Don't—" Don't call me that. If you call me that, I might as well be him.

"I love you, Jules." His hard-on was obvious against Julian's thigh. A little nudge and they were side by side, both equally hard. Quin looked like he might cry, and for the first time, seeing his face like that awakened something other than irritation or indifference in Julian.

"God help me, I love you too," he whispered, ground himself against Quin and bit him on the neck.

The chime on the door startled him back from his heat. Quin slid down to the floor behind the counter. Shit. Who the f—?

Julian hurried to button and straighten his waistcoat. He glanced at the door where an unpleasantly familiar figure was wiping his hat and the moist lapels of his suit. The man set his hat on the side table.

"Mr Ballroth. What brings you by, sir?" Julian suffered to retrieve the remnants of his service smile.

"Has the young master reconsidered my offer? I am willing to negotiate a higher price for the building." The man wiped his greasy forehead with a stained handkerchief.

Julian looked away. Quin sat on the floor below him, watching him, trying to steady his ragged breathing so as not to make noise.

It took all Julian had to not tell Mr Ballroth to go fuck himself.

"The young master is unwell today, sir."

"Oh? How unfortunate. These old houses can be hazardous to one's health. It would be wise of him to vacate while he still can." The putrid penguin wobbled across the room undeterred.

Julian had expected Quin to jump at the chance to make things uncomfortable and weird behind the counter, but when Julian glanced down, he sat there obediently, waiting and watching him back like a wide-eyed fawn.

Shit. This uncharacteristic obedience was worse, wasn't it? Julian despaired. How could he get rid of the disgusting numps prancing around, yapping about wanting to buy the place, to get back to what they had been doing before the rude interruption?

Shit, shit! Was that a yawn? Quin had a single tear in one corner of his eye. The mood was already wrecked, that much was obvious... But what if it was soon wrecked beyond repair?

"Can you relay my newest offer to Mr Wakefield? I have a substantial increase in mind that is sure to perk his interest!"

I will fucking *perk* your substantial cane into your fucking ass if you don't have the wits to get lost this instant! Julian gritted his teeth.

There was another yawn at his feet as the insufferable dimwit continued to make his case, listing reasons such as costly renovations and the value of the area plummeting to entice his wholly deaf audience.

Julian gripped the edge of the counter in absolute agony. Quin had closed his eyes. This was no time to fall asleep sitting! Julian tried to nudge him with his foot, and, for a moment, he looked alert but quickly seemed to doze off again.

"I can come back tomorrow if that would suit better—"

"For the love of the Guardian, piss off! No one wants to sell! It's not for sale!" Julian stormed around the counter and scooped Mr Ballroth swiftly toward the door.

"But, but, but, but, but surely—!"

"Get the f— out of my sight!" He threw the man's hat after him, slammed the door and, once he'd calmed down somewhat, turned the sign to indicate the pharmacy was closed.

Quin? He tried to peek over the counter, then hurried to check from the side.

"Quin?"

"Hmm?" Quin turned to look at Julian at the corner of the counter, stretched his arms wide and yawned. A sharp sting interrupted him mid-yawn. "Ow."

"Are you all right?"

"Is it ripped? Can you check?"

Julian knelt next to him and leaned closer.

"It looks a little red, but it's not bleeding. You seem tired…"

"No, don't worry about it. Can you pull me up?" He was used to running, but he'd tried a new hillier and longer route today for some added challenge.

After not being able to work out as much as he was accustomed to because of his injuries, it felt great to be able to run again, but he was a little out of shape and his knees were definitely feeling the strain.

"Maybe we should—" Julian hoisted him to his feet.

"Continue where we left off?" Quin made an aggressive effort to stifle his yawn.

He heard the faint sound of a cough. Julian turned to look toward the stairs. The cough was followed by some sounds of shuffling and a few thumping footsteps, but Rhys didn't get very far before Julian had caught him at the lower half of the stairs.

"Aren't you supposed to be resting?" Julian had grabbed him by the hem of his shirt.

"I was going to, in a minute!" Rhys turned to Quin. "I'm sorry. I didn't mean to disturb you."

Julian let go of his shirt and only then seemed to realise what all Rhys must have overheard. His cheeks were slowly turning crimson, and his brow furrowed.

"It's OK. It wouldn't have mattered if not for Mr Let-me-buy-the-place butting in." Quin instinctively massaged Julian's arm to get him to relax. "But maybe you really should get some rest, Rhys. You look like you might be getting a fever." Quin reached over to test Rhys's forehead. Rhys waved his hand away.

"It's not a fever." He gave Quin a sharp look. After a brief awkward silence, he added, "I'm going to go rest, but if you've got some unfinished business, don't mind me. It's fine."

"Would it be OK if we used Julian's room?" Quin asked tentatively. There was no way sounds wouldn't carry over to Rhys's.

"Yes, that's perfectly fine."

Julian seemed taken aback, but Quin was too amused not to laugh.

"I'll try to be discreet."

"Don't bother." Rhys turned around and started climbing up the stairs.

"Should I not be discreet, then?" Quin called after him. His words were met with a negligent wave of a hand.

"Quin!" Julian grabbed him by the arm.

"Relax, it's fine. He clearly likes it."

There was something oddly satisfying about having an appreciative audience, albeit one a little too shy to admit it openly.

"But I don't!" Julian glared at him.

What a bloody liar. Quin chuckled.

"Would you rather I get washed up first, or do you want me dirty today?" He smiled. As soon as he did, Julian reacted with his usual aggravated deflection; it definitely still had the desired effect on him.

"Get yourself sorted. You stink."

"Are you sure? A warm bath might make me sleepy." Quin made a point to yawn.

"Damn it, Quin. Stop pushing my buttons. I'll do it to you both before and after and all the way 'til you pass out."

"Is that a promise?" Quin purred from the thought. "What about during...?"

THE CATNAP FUMBLERS - PRIVATE AFTERWORDS

CHAPTER 7

Quin was about to enter the bathroom to get washed when Julian pushed him in there with enough force to almost make him fall over. He looked back with some apprehension but was relieved to see Julian follow in behind him. He grinned, gripped Julian by the shirt to pull him closer, and gave him his customary tongue greeting.

"You're filthy."

"I know."

"Get in there." Julian grabbed him by the hair to drag him over to the bathtub.

"Clothes?"

"Fuck the clothes." Julian turned on the faucet. Cold water washed over Quin's hair and crept down the back of his shirt. Julian held him under the shower, with water spilling into his eyes and mouth, making him feel even more at his mercy.

"You said you would fuck me before I get washed," Quin complained.

Julian opened the front of his trousers and pulled them, as well as his underpants, down and off him.

Quin tried to kiss him, but the man forced him against the wall. He tried his luck leaning forward, but he was stuck there, rendered immobile to avoid a bald patch, with water still dripping into his eyes and mouth from the shower head above.

"I knew you were still in there, Jules." Quin bestowed one of his smirks on Julian.

Julian eyed him and tightened his grip on the hair. He looked the same as he used to when he was waiting for an excuse to let all hell break loose. Quin obliged by collecting some water in his mouth and spitting it in his face.

In a split second, Julian pulled him forth and slammed him against the wall, eyes burning with anger. When he tried to kiss Quin, Quin bit his tongue hard enough to be sure it hurt.

It was like old times! He couldn't help but laugh as Julian flung him across the room, yet pulled him back in to grab his ass when he noticed it was within his reach. Quin laughed. Julian pinched him.

"Ow, shit..." That would leave a mark.

It was a challenge to relieve Julian of his clothes, but after tumbling through the bathroom and pinning him momentarily between the door and the shelf, the trousers were off.

Half of his shirt lay on the floor as the first clear casualty, but Quin could afford to reimburse it if the new Julian was pettier than the old.

He latched himself onto Julian's waist and hung on to dear life as he was hoisted across the room again until they hit the opposing wall. This was when the blessed man finally grabbed the bottle of petroleum jelly off the shelf, slapped some on his dick and drove it into Quin's ass.

He was a little out of practice, but it went in without any further injuries. Quin sunk his nails into Julian's back and moaned. Julian had always appreciated instant feedback, and would get down to business more promptly with this encouragement.

"Ah, don't spare me." Quin made himself comfortable. The pain from being roughed up was soon replaced by the intense arousal he'd missed for over a decade. Tears streamed down his face as he welcomed the euphoria.

"You're a sick man," Julian whispered, his voice hoarse from growling and his breath ragged from the exercise.

"I know." Quin kissed him unreservedly. A respectable number of thrusts later, he could feel Julian cum inside of him, and he was already filled with regret that it was ending so soon.

"Why do you do this to yourself?" Julian slowed down to stroke his hair. Technically he was the one doing it, but it was true Julian had always offered him a way out. Quin played this game fully willing, even if his banged up body was now paying the price.

"Why do you put up with me? You should have slapped some sense into me..." Julian seemed sad. He held his hand at Quin's cheek and gave him a careful, tender kiss. "I'm s—"

Quin lifted his finger to Julian's lips to hush him.

"We've talked about this. You don't say that."

"Did I hurt you?" Julian helped Quin up to stand.

"Ow, ow, ow..." Quin could tell he wasn't going to be going for another run any time soon. His ribs had only just stopped hurting, but the pain was now back as bad as ever. He leaned on the wall to try to catch his breath without breathing in too deeply.

"Shit, no. This is not right. I'm sor—"

"Don't say it." Quin shut his mouth with his full hand this time. "You'll make me feel bad. I'm as much to blame if not more. I just need a minute..." He felt precariously close to fainting, but he'd be damned if he let Julian take the fall for something he'd instigated.

"Let's get you washed up. Does it hurt? I'll give you something so you can get some rest."

"You promised me during and after!" Quin reminded him and straightened himself up.

"I'm going to have to make it up to you later."

"At least during... I'm not done yet!"

"I'm s—"

"Oh no, you don't. You can't leave me hanging with this..." He was dripping, hard and ready to go. He didn't expect Julian to go for it, but it was one of those things he needed to say out loud for his own peace of mind.

"Let's get you washed up. I'll wash you," Julian offered.

"What?" What was that last part? You'll wash me up? Like just now, or...? Quin stared at him with his mouth agape.

Julian helped him out of his wet shirt, told him to sit on the side of the bathtub and started washing him with a sponge.

"Ah—" Quin seized him by the wrist when he was about to lather his privates with it. He'd only just managed to settle down, almost.

"Everywhere." Julian eyed him sternly. One look at those eyes and Quin was hard again. He watched Julian wash every part of him in disbelief and some resentment for not getting relief and having to struggle to breathe without pain.

The bathroom was in shambles. It was strange that no one had come in to check what was going on. But then again, Quin realised, maybe they had but he'd failed to notice. It's not like he'd paid attention to anything but Julian for the past however many minutes.

"Who's going to clean this up?"

Quin closed his eyes, exhausted. Julian had rinsed him and was now drying him with a towel. What a strange after service he had not seen coming.

"I'll deal with it tomorrow. Can you stand?"

"Of course I can." Quin propped himself up. His sides were stinging and aching, and he felt bruised all over. Pre-existing half-healed injuries were no fun whatsoever! This should have been nothing. Maybe he was getting old?

"Come on then." Julian escorted him out of what was left of the bathroom.

"Will you be sleeping with Rhys tonight?"

"No. He needs to rest. I'll be in my own room."

"Can I?" It was worth at least asking, even if the sex was already more than he'd dared to hope for.

Julian glanced at him and sighed.

"Sit down. I'll go get my kit."

Sit down, where? The nearest place was on the sofa in the lounge. He wobbled over there and lowered himself to sit.

What a depressing end to a promising evening. Rhys had been right to warn him about getting carried away.

Julian returned upstairs with his kit. He checked Quin's ribs, decided on the dose and deposited the drops on Quin's tongue. It had a familiar acrid taste. Quin winced.

"Do you want something to wash it down with?" Julian packed away his kit and got up.

"If you're offering."

"I'll brew you a cup of chamomile."

Quin stared at Julian making him a cup of herbal tea with a keen sense he had left this world to an alternate reality.

"Did you give me that stuff from the willow bark again?" It hadn't tasted the same, but Quin didn't dare to hope.

"It was laudanum. But I'm going to lock you into the coal cellar if you start pinching it from my inventory." He offered Quin the cup of tea.

"Oh, thank Guardian. I really am not feeling great..." The tea tasted nice. It was too hot to drink more than a tiny sip at a time, though.

"Well?"

"Well what?"

"I thought you wanted to sleep in my room."

"You'll let me?"

"You'll be sedated in just a bit, so it's not like I'll need to wrestle with you for the space."

Quin perked up, although in a moderate, careful manner. He got up, making sure not to spill his drink, and followed Julian across the hall very, very slowly.

"Quin?" Rhys peeked from his bedroom.

"Huh?" Quin lifted his eyes off the cup.

"Are you all right?"

"Couldn't be better."

"Will you stay up for long?" Rhys directed his question to Julian.

"No. Sorry we disturbed you. We'll be quiet from now on."

"That's all right. Are we sure he's OK?"

"He's banged up, but he should be fine with some rest."

They were talking about him like he wasn't even there. Quin stared at the cup in his hand and realised why. Ah, so nice. It no longer hurt to breathe! Julian took the cup from his hands and guided him towards the bedroom.

"Sit down." Julian set the teacup on the windowsill and put away his robe to change into his nightshirt.

Quin lay on the bed with his legs hanging over the side and his robe wide open.

"Julian."

What an indecent sight. Julian avoided looking.

"Jules."

"Go to sleep."

"Jules..." Quin stretched his arm out to him. "Please come to bed with me." He looked pitiful in that state. Laudanum was not the top choice due to its myriad of side effects if the dose wasn't right or it was used too often, but at least Quin seemed to be making the best of its benefits. He lay there heedless with his dick out, relaxed but seeking attention.

"Fine." Julian lifted Quin's legs on the bed and sat on the side so he could lean down to give him a kiss.

"Please don't leave me hanging..." Quin ran his fingertips across Julian's bare chest. It was surprising to see him still in the mood for more.

"You're not in a state to continue, love. I'll try not to lose my temper next time," Julian whispered.

"No, no, no..." Quin objected lazily. "You can do it to me any time. I just need to heal first."

"That's not going to be for a while. And we can't keep wrecking the bathroom. I'll learn to do it in a way you'll still enjoy. I just need some more practice controlling myself." He felt sick recalling how rough he'd got from being both turned on and enraged at the same time. "We should hold off until I figure it out. It's strange. I can usually manage myself with Rhys, but as soon as it's you, I lose my mind."

"I prefer it that way. You're gorgeous when you're mad with rage. I'm sorry I keep pissing you off intentionally... I just can't help myself." Quin let his arms fall aside. The drug seemed to be getting a proper hold of him now. "Can you kiss me, Jules? I'm too tired to move."

Julian leaned in lower to humour him. The least he could do was try to make Quin comfortable. He massaged Quin's penis until the man was groaning and moaning with no filter. He seemed adamant to hang in there to not let it end as soon as it could have, so Julian entertained his wish by giving him moments to pause, to edge him slowly closer and to let him enjoy it until it looked like he might pass out.

"You need to sleep, love." Julian kissed him.

"No— ah, no, please..."

"Don't worry, I won't leave you hanging."

"Jules... I love you... Please..." Quin looked pained. If he wasn't going to surrender by hand, Julian was fairly sure he would not last for long in his mouth.

As expected, Quin tensed up and, surprised by the turn of events, seemed like he would try to escape. Julian pressed him gently down by the abdomen to remind him not to hurt himself. Then he sucked his dick until Quin released his load and collapsed into a drowsy heap of incoherent mumbles. Julian swallowed to avoid the hassle of a cleanup.

"You should sleep." He patted Quin's head, amused by the incessant love confessions and rambling slurring out of Quin's mouth. It reminded him of himself when he'd been euphoric dreamside with Rhys for the first time. If it was even half as nice for Quin right now, then perhaps the man would forgive being used as a punching bag...

No, that was no excuse. Quin deserved better.

"Next time, I want us to skip the injuries and go straight to this part. All right? Without the laudanum, though. You seem too out of it to fully enjoy it."

"It's fine the way it is. You feel better, don't you?" Quin clung to Julian's nightshirt. It was true he'd felt inexplicably calm right after he'd emptied his load into Quin, but that was no excuse... "I'm usually more durable than this."

Julian was about to object.

"I'm fine so long as you don't leave me hanging."

"Keep reminding me if I forget."

"Come to bed, Jules."

"I need to brush my teeth, but I'll be right there." Julian got up. Quin hung on to his fingers for a while before reluctantly letting go. When Julian returned, he was asleep.

CHAPTER 8

Summer on Whitskersey was in full swing, with the preparations for the Midsummer Festival coming to an end after keeping Vincent and the rest of the tight-knit island community busy for the past few months.

Because Jasmine had begged Julian to enrol her in a private boarding school in Chattsmouth to prepare herself for her role as the pharmacist's apprentice, she seemed especially determined to make the best of her last free summer before her studies, and Ren seemed happy to oblige her.

This excitement and talk about going to a boarding school had sparked some conversation and caused a rift between Ren, Vincent and Celandine concerning Ren's education.

Ren was a year younger than Jasmine, but she had been buttering up and pestering Vincent to let her go, too, to study to become a doctor or a scientist like Aurora.

It didn't seem like a bad idea, but Vincent admittedly worried about how well Ren would adjust to a big-city school after only ever going to the one on the island. It also meant she would move to Chattsmouth—where the Girl's College of Science, Aurora's alma mater, was located—fairly far away from both Whitskersey and Schadesborough.

Vincent was leaning towards letting her go, since, as per his calculations, he could just about afford it without having to scour to collect his remaining dues, and it seemed like a wonderful opportunity for her. She'd already have a friend and a more stable environment while Vincent crisscrossed the country with Aurora in search of new information on the Guardian.

It would be no trouble at all to stop by for frequent visits in case Ren felt terribly homesick and to make sure she was doing all right.

Celandine voiced a slew of worries and objections, and while some of them were justified, most were based on her outdated, and frankly silly, opinions. She was highly in favour of education, but her suspicions and deeply-rooted prejudice against science were difficult to dispel.

The islanders were on average more open towards scientific advances than the mainlanders, mainly because they had experienced first-hand how much of a difference they could make to the standard of living, especially when stuck on a wintry arctic island for half the year.

Some of the more restrictive religious doctrines hadn't gained much traction here, where people still casually worshipped Holy Maury, the mother of the Sea and Weaver of the waves. Even so, they were far from comfortable with anything outside the daily practicalities such as snowtrains, ploughs and the newest medicine for chests and colds.

Celandine had tolerated Vincent's interest in mechanics because it had kept him out of trouble most days. Ren was unjustly expected not to get in trouble in the first place, simply due to her gender.

She was also expected to get an education, but, in Celandine's mind, this should have been something more traditionally suitable for a girl like becoming a nurse or a governess.

Having had the pleasure of watching Aurora work, Vincent was convinced there was nothing whatsoever wrong with aspiring to become a scientist. He was prepared to have a screaming match with Celandine so she could feel like she'd done her part in convincing them to drop the foolish idea. He was merely putting it off because he wasn't sure whether Ren should wait another year before going. She seemed awfully young to be sent alone to a boarding school. That, and he'd been busy lately, completing his second book, finishing up some upgrades to his speeder, and helping out with the Festival preparations.

The Midsummer Festival had never seemed as fascinating to Vincent as it did on the morning of the first day.

It was a four-day event which, in Vincent's tired eyes, had always seemed too noisy, too bustling and generally overwhelming for his senses. Likewise, he'd avoided taking on responsibilities in the preparations like one would avoid a rat-infested ship, but it felt good to take part in it, for once, without having to feign enthusiasm.

The market square was decorated with garlands of flowers, colourful paper and fabric ornaments. There was a small raised stage in the middle, where the dancers gave performances in honour of Holy Maury. Treats and trinkets were sold in the stalls, and there were competitions being held for traditional summer games as well as craftsmanship and gardening.

Vincent had participated once or twice in the past, but after he'd lost most of his tools, half of his garden and his greenhouse in the fire, he'd assumed he'd only be watching this year. Not only had they roped him into helping out with the assembly of the stalls and decorations, the governor was hounding him about judging some of the many competitions scheduled for the next four days.

Vincent was happy to participate, but not that happy. He wasn't dead set against acting as a judge; he just would've much rather watched the dancers dance and soaked up the atmosphere now that they seemed like something he might have the energy to appreciate.

He'd had a full night's sleep nearly every other night the week prior. On the nights he woke up once or twice, all he had to do was make a brief conscious effort, and he could make himself fall asleep again. The amount of restful sleep he'd had in the past half a year felt like more than he'd had in his whole life.

Writing the second book had been a breeze. The speeder was in such good shape, he was tempted to take a mallet to hack it to pieces to have something more to do to it. He'd learned all the people's names and remembered most of the things they told him. He hardly ever felt hopelessly confused while having a casual conversation with someone, and he found himself capable of taking genuine interest in them instead of grasping at a semblance of good manners to avoid being hated.

There was only one problem, really.

Just one tiny, massive problem he was having amongst all this, as he watched Ren and Jasmine run around the market square and Aurora trailing after them, trying to rein them in a little.

All this would have been relaxing and idyllic if not for this one miniscule, gargantuan problem.

Aurora waved to him from across the market square, more beautiful than any of the decorations or the dancers up on their platform.

Vincent had spent the past few months in a frustrating limbo with no opportunity for privacy and no progress in their relationship. He'd never thought of himself as an impatient man or expected to want to send Ren away for a while. Because of their past, he couldn't bear to make such a request even if she likely wouldn't have minded spending a day or two in town with Celandine so long as she had Jasmine to keep her company.

After exchanging a few words with Ren and Jasmine, Aurora headed his way. For a split-second, Vincent felt an urge to run away. He looked around for an excuse, but if he left this secluded spot between two stalls, he ran the risk of bumping into the governor. There didn't seem to be a safe direction to run to without getting dragged to the judging tables.

"Are you looking for someone?" Aurora had hurried enough to sound out of breath. "If I didn't know any better, I'd think you were looking for an escape just now."

"No, of course not!" That would have technically counted as leaving her, and he'd sincerely promised not to. He'd also privately sworn not to lie to her, so he hung his head in shame. "I might have..."

"What's wrong?"

He hadn't meant to worry her, and to prevent it from getting any worse, he pulled her behind one of the stalls to explain. She looked further startled.

"I'm not sure," he confessed. That was why the situation was so difficult to navigate. He'd never had to deal with something like this. He'd been busy surviving and not drawing attention to himself.

"Are you having trouble sleeping? Do you feel sick?" Aurora seemed about to test him for fever, so he took her hands in his.

"No, that's not it. I'm sleeping fine. I'm just feeling restless. Like I can't concentrate."

"Maybe the connection is still malfunctioning? It might be causing some unusual strain—"

"I don't think that's it." Vincent placed his thumb on her lips. "It only happens when you're here."

"Oh..." She frowned. "Do you need me to go?"

"No, no. Of course not. I don't need to concentrate. I don't—"

Something about her presence was messing with his head. He'd tried to ignore it, but all he wanted to do since Midwinter's Eve was to kiss her over and over, obsessively.

Her lips felt soft under his thumb, but he knew if he kissed her now, it would only get worse. It was already getting worse, and there were people around. The stall provided some cover from prying eyes, but it was hardly private.

"Do you need me to do something?" Aurora moved his hand away.

"No." He leaned in closer to hug her, even if that, too, was only going to make it more torturous.

"Are you sure you're all right? You don't seem yourself. Whatever it is, we'll figure it out."

"I'm frustrated."

"Why?"

"You know." He felt childish even saying it. At his age, he should have had a better handle on himself. But how was he supposed to, really, when he'd had almost no practice? He'd never had to curb urges like these. He'd been much too tired, even when he'd been younger and healthier.

"We have time. You just need to wait a while longer," she whispered into his ear. Her hair smelled fresh and floral.

"How long?" Vincent closed his eyes and took in the scent. Rosemary with a hint of violet.

"There's still plenty of time before we need to take the girls to their new school."

The Whitskersey summer wasn't long, but it might as well have been an eternity the way it dragged on. It was the first day of the Midsummer Festival for crying out loud! He was never going to last all the way to September. While thinking this, half of his mind was searching through his memory for a suitable boat shed or a fenced yard to sneak into, for even the tiniest taste of her.

When he opened his eyes, she was looking at him, worried.

He looks so pained. I thought he was hoping Celandine would approve, but... maybe he's not ready to let Ren go to that school yet. Maybe I should try to talk her out of it.

"No, hell no." At least with Ren going to Chattsmouth, there was a cut-off point to this torture.

"What?"

"That's not why I'm frustrated."

"Oh?" Aurora frowned. *Then why? Oh. He doesn't strike me as the type—*

"I didn't think I'd be like this myself. I don't know what's wrong with me. It's never been like this before."

He was continuously one stray thought away from having to adjust his trousers. Not even in his teens had he been this excitable or sensitive. It felt like blood might rush through his body from the smallest of things, and, while that burst of energy didn't feel bad in itself, having to stay on guard and try to curb it did.

Perhaps the boat shed would be his best option? But it wasn't particularly romantic, and Vincent wasn't sure whether Aurora wanted to wait to make their intimate reunion special somehow.

Should he excuse himself and take care of it somewhere on his own like the countless times before? But the governor was lurking out there, ready to strike at the sight of him.

"Hmm. Could it be a delayed hormonal awakening now that your body is finally getting enough rest to function properly? Or are you just not used to being fully awake?"

He'd felt inadequate and small in the face of her theorising before, but after busying himself by reading whatever scientific literature he could get his hands on, her words no longer sounded foreign. He didn't have to strain himself trying to understand her. He was free to enjoy what she was saying and how she said it.

Better not. She looked him in the eye, but it was brief.

"No, I think you'd better," he said.

She blushed. *I wish he'd said that the last time.* She reached up to kiss him.

"Vincent! There you are. I have been looking for you. We are about to start with the assorted crafts category." The governor appeared as if by infernal intervention and caused Vincent to scream inwardly.

There was some consolation in the fact that Aurora had thought of some rather poignant, unbecoming words at that precise moment, so Vincent wasn't the only one irked by the interruption.

He barely had time to say, "I'm so sorry," before he was forced to leave her.

CHAPTER 9

To Julian's surprise, Rhys hadn't reminded him about the promise to reverse positions dreamside. Part of it was likely because he'd been down with a cold for close to two weeks, so he'd needed to rest. But it was well into summer now with no mention of it, so Julian wondered if the boy had forgotten.

Almost exactly six months from when it had been mentioned, and just as Julian had begun to think he might not have to do it, Rhys finally brought it up dreamside.

The days leading up to it had been busy. Julian had gone to Grymswich, Gobehurst and Firth for supplies, by himself, and returned after seven days of heated negotiations with the different herbalists, chemists and medical engineers.

To say that he was tired was an understatement. He was tempted to tell Rhys no, but since something had kept him from asking earlier, and he'd opened his mouth now, Julian couldn't bring himself to let the boy down.

"If it's a bad timing, I guess we could—"

"No, I promised, and it's long overdue."

Julian had tried not to think about it too deeply. He'd experimented with some alterations while Rhys was not there, to see how it would feel. It hadn't been great. He'd never truly know how Rhys felt, but he'd gained a slightly better grasp of it.

Even so, he'd made a promise.

"All right, well, we should probably head out of here, then." Rhys offered him a hand.

"What? Where?" Julian stared at the hand.

"Over to my side." Rhys took his hand and started to feel for the edge of the bubble.

"Why? I'm sorry. I'm a little tired, I don't follow..."

"The Guardian seems to connect me to you when I'm in your bubble, so I can feel what you're feeling. When I mentioned it to Hosta—not in the same context, obviously—she explained it's what's called a 'diagnostics function'. Its job is to provide data so it's easier to diagnose any issues in the system. So, by coming here, the Guardian supplies me with your sensory input. Because I didn't know how it felt to touch myself or to have an erection, it didn't feel like much to me. Now that I know, it's significantly better."

"So," Julian tortured his tired brain cells to put it together, "you want me to jump over so I can get your 'sensory input'?"

"Yes."

Ah, there was a tiny inkling of recognition as to why Rhys had been stalling with this. Perhaps there was something there that he'd hesitated to share.

"Unless you want to back out? It's likely to alter your mental state a little, although it probably won't be as overwhelming as your bubble feels to me when you get distracted. But I understand if you don't want to be subjected to it..."

"That's fine. It's only fair."

"Are you sure?"

"Yes. It can't be worse than what you have to put up with here." Because Rhys was still off by several inches, Julian guided his hands to where the edge of the bubble was. He wasn't looking forward to jumping through the void, but he was curious about what was waiting on the other side.

"Do not let go of my hand!" The boy tightened his grip and pulled Julian along.

It had been a while since Justin had done this, but it was impossible to forget the feeling of hitting a wall of icy shards, being sucked into it and compressed from all sides at once with such force Julian wondered if he was going to implode.

He was yanked through until the resistance lessened abruptly, and he nearly fell on his face.

"Holy sh—" He struggled to regain his balance and find his feet. Everything was so soft and airy here! Where was this? What—?

"Are you all right?" Rhys turned around to check on him.

"I'm fine, but how is it so *big*? It's so vast! Where is this?"

"This is where I sleep." Rhys shrugged. "Make yourself comfortable."

Yes, but how and where? Julian felt nearly weightless walking through what seemed like a light version of reality with no physical boundaries.

What was this feeling? Whatever it was, it felt like it was seeping right through into him. Uhhh...

"What is this?" Julian turned to look at Rhys to make sense of the odd fluffiness he was feeling. Rhys was standing right in front of him. What a peculiar expression. He couldn't quite catch up. Was it because he was tired? Was it this space? Something was messing with his senses...

Oh.

Rhys kissed him. Right. This was what they were here for. So sweet, so soft... but for the moment it lasted, it grounded him firmly where he stood. He was fine. This was probably just the sensory input Rhys had mentioned.

"Do you know how to change it? Do you need help?" Rhys moved his hand to where Julian was already hard.

Julian had tried it before, but he wasn't sure if he'd done it right, and it seemed like it might be more difficult with an erection. Where was that supposed to go or fit? He nodded.

"I need help..."

"Close your eyes. I think I might be able to do it for you here."

"Oh?" Good. That was good.

Uhhhh. He struggled to concentrate. He closed his eyes, but it only made the feeling spreading through his body even more pronounced.

Nothing seemed to happen but something did. It was so subtle that if it hadn't been for this silky softness messing with his head and making him more aware of his body, he likely would have missed it.

Rhys set his hand on Julian's cheek.

"Are you ready?"

"Yes, sure." It wasn't as unpleasant as he'd thought. He felt mostly normal.

"Are you sure?"

Julian opened his eyes to Rhys grinning. It was unsettling enough for him to reconsider. Was he missing something? Uhhhh... This feeling was so distracting.

"Do you feel it?" Rhys whispered.

"Yes... What is it?"

"It's me. Hello, and welcome." He smiled and gave Julian another kiss, this time much more indulgent than the previous one. The softness wrapped around Julian and squeezed every part of him. Something inside of him was thrumming subtly.

As he kissed Rhys back, he felt a warm ache somewhere within his lower abdomen, and the thrum grew into more of an oscillating pressure. Uhhhhhhh...

Rhys slipped his hand into Julian's breeches, and the ease with which the hand fit in confirmed to Julian that the shape had indeed changed.

He knew it was temporary and that his dick hadn't disappeared for good, but knowing it wasn't there after so many years—especially when it was supposed to be there in its full erect glory—was unsettling. He was about to interject when Rhys slid his fingers over his mound and between the labia.

It wasn't so much the sensation of something touching him down there as it was Rhys's face when he did it: his eyes bright and that borderline lecherous grin as he moved his fingers; on any other person, Julian would have found it off-putting, but because it was Rhys, he was brimming with curiosity.

Rhys seemed to be having trouble breathing right. Usually he wouldn't respond like this until much later when he was finally getting more comfortable and into the mood, but he—

"Why is this so *hot*?" He seemed like he was lusting for it.

"What?"

"I hate this thing, but when it's you, it's so... I want to... I have this urge to..." He was fingering the front like he was wanting to pry it open but barely restraining himself.

The warm fingers against the unfamiliar shapes felt strange but pleasant. Tempted to let the boy explore further but unnerved that he might just decide to forgo any preparations—if such were relevant dreamside—Julian stopped Rhys.

Rhys frowned. "Do you want to back out? Is it uncomfortable?"

Ah, thank the Guardian, you are still level-headed enough to care, Julian thought. If this overwhelming soft confusion was coming from Rhys, he seemed to not be in his right mind. It begged the question why.

Was he drunk? Why was he in such a state?

"No, I'm just a little worried. You don't seem yourself," Julian explained.

Maybe it was because they had been separated for a couple of days? Had something happened while Julian had been away? Rhys had seemed normal when he'd come home, though.

"Ah, sorry." Rhys hugged him. "It's the time of the month I feel most into this, you know? I've been waiting for you to come home. I've missed you."

As their bodies bumped together, it was obvious Rhys was hard. It seemed somehow even more obvious when Julian had nothing to match it with like usual.

The throbbing feeling was all the more distracting, though, because it wasn't contained like it was supposed to be. It felt like there should have been something there for the blood to run into, and it was building pressure at such an unusual place, Julian struggled to identify what or why it was happening.

It's to be expected, he told himself. It was probably meant to feel weird. It would give him insight into how Rhys experienced sex when they were awake, and understanding that would be valuable insight indeed.

But.

And there was a big but.

"I'm starting to get too tired to hold it in."

Rhys pulled back from his hug to look at Julian.

"My inside thoughts. I feel like I might start rambling," Julian clarified.

To be fair, he'd been using a lot of his concentration the past few days negotiating prices and making sure he was buying everything he needed. Some of the Grymswich herbalists were enthusiastic hecklers and made an obscure ritual out of it. Travelling in itself was taxing.

"I don't mind if you do. You know that, right?" Rhys held Julian's cheek as if caressing a delicate, fair maiden, and Julian had to wonder if he had changed any other parts besides the genitals.

"I wish I had a mirror."

"What?"

"Ah, see. My mind is wandering. It's so difficult to concentrate here. My insides feel like marmalade. Did you make me look somehow different? You seem taller."

"No, I just adjusted the relevant parts, but you do seem a little smaller." He traced Julian's ear and the side of his hair with his fingers.

To think of it, Julian was standing straight, but Rhys was at his eye-level, and that simply shouldn't have been possible.

"Oh, maybe the system is simulating how the changes would affect you in real life? Could be part of the diagnostics toolkit."

"You've spent too much time with my mother..."

Julian realised he wasn't really even at eye-level! He was having to look up at Rhys, albeit not by much. For whatever reason, this made him feel even worse than missing his dick.

"I've been a complete ass!"

"Huh?"

"I didn't realise it was like this."

He'd been treating Rhys like a kid without understanding his height had nothing to do with it. He was still mentally calling Rhys 'a boy'. He was not a boy. He was obviously a grown man. Julian had thought he'd understood this, but clearly he hadn't.

"Can we stop talking? I'm trying my hardest to give you space to adjust, and I don't mean to pressure you, but you need to call it off right now or let me do something. I need to do something." Rhys snuggled back closer and pressed his cheek against Julian's. He was warm. The strange, bothersome feeling inside Julian had waned somewhat, but it was quickly returning.

"Go easy on me." Julian wasn't about to back out. Rhys had put up with this for him, so it was high time to return the favour.

"Don't worry. It'll still feel good. You made it feel good for me." Rhys kissed Julian's neck. Julian shivered. With increasingly mixed feelings, he thought back to the times they'd had sex the past six months and the absolute state in which Rhys had been each of those times. Was that where this was heading?

He'd given this enough thought to imagine the raw gist of it, but he'd assumed it would be more like it always was, with him being him, save for what was down there, and them fooling around in the confines of his bubble.

This place was so vast and airy it made him feel light-headed and fluff-brained like he was wrapped in the softest luxury goose down. He couldn't concentrate for the weird throbbing feeling down there.

"Well, I knew it's supposed to feel like something, but why is it so bloody vague and spread out? What is in there?"

"Well," Rhys opened the front of his pyjamas. "I'm hoping it'll soon be this." He seemed proud of himself.

Julian wanted to groan, but considering this was Rhys, and he seemed genuinely excited, he was too cute to be mad at. His dick was nothing but, though.

"How is it so *big*?" A sense of déjà vu crept up on Julian. "That's not going to fit."

"What? Sure it will. It's the perfect size. Made it myself." Rhys grinned.

"I guess you're the expert—" Julian bit his lip and tried to focus. At least his own wasn't currently visible for comparison, because if that thing was bigger... Sword fight aside, it felt like a subtle criticism that Julian could have stood to be bigger to fully satisfy Rhys when they were awake.

"Don't worry about it. I know what to do. Just relax."

"Easier said than done—"

Julian was still worried about his implied lacklustre size when Rhys interrupted him with another kiss and pushed him down on the floor. Then he pulled down Julian's breeches while kissing his abdomen. What it lacked in seductive romantics, it was providing amply with enthusiasm.

Julian yelped.

That was Rhys's tongue between his labia.

A little bit of seduction first wouldn't have gone amiss! Uhhhhhhhh. The tongue was still there. Julian gasped.

Something was dripping. Saliva? No?

"Aaaah...!" Fuck. That actually felt nice, but it made him feel restless and uncomfortable at the same time. Oh. He recognised this move. He'd done this to Rhys. Oh no. "A—! Aaaaahhhh!"

So this was what it felt like?

"It's a good thing we're not awake because that would have definitely woken Quin and Victor." Rhys lifted his face from his feast, visibly amused. "I wouldn't outright turn down a foursome, but the logistics give me a headache, and I'm not in the mood for anything complicated. Oh, look! It is wet already!" He rubbed the opening gently with his finger.

"I see what you meant about not needing narration."

"It's a little more tricky to know the right timing when I don't feel it myself, so your feedback is very helpful." Rhys pushed the finger in.

"Ah, this doesn't feel right." Julian had had time to refresh some old memories with Quin, but this was not the same. It went in much too easily without adding lubrication, yet it seemed like a worryingly snug fit, like something might rip.

Julian regretted any of the times he'd been impatient with Rhys because the fear the man might just ram his dick in there without proper preparations was intense.

One moment it felt like this might be something he could get into, and the next, he was terrified Rhys might get carried away.

"Don't worry, I was just testing it for myself. I'm not going to thrust myself in like some asshole last time..." Rhys's grin was back. He withdrew the finger.

"I'm sorry!" Julian usually made sure to take his time, but there had been a night a few days before his departure to Grymswich when he'd had a little too much to drink, and instead of spending the night with Quin like he'd intended, he'd ended up with Rhys... He'd not been out of his mind drunk, but his self-control had been more lacking than usual.

"It's OK. You looked like you were enjoying yourself. I've been thinking about it ever since. Like, what I would do to you, when I got the chance. But don't worry, this is not revenge. I just want to know what it's like."

"Well, you could also do me in the ass—" Julian frowned and closed his eyes. "I didn't mean to suggest that out loud, but... You could, I suppose. To skip this step of turning me into a woman."

"Sure, I'll do you in any way you want, later, but can we get back to this? Since it's there, and we're here already." He made himself comfortable and sunk his tongue back between the labia. His mouth was so velvety and warm, Julian throbbed.

"Uhhhhhhhh... Ahhhhh..."

"It feels good, doesn't it? I've been experimenting a little. It seems it requires a lot of time to get it to respond, but I found a way to get around that somewhat." As he spoke, he resumed work with his fingers.

"Aah... haah... How?"

"You felt it when you came here, right?" Rhys slipped his finger in again, and it went in like a knife through warm butter.

"Hnnnnnhhhh... Aaaaaah... Yessss..."

"I primed *it* before you came in, to save us some time."

What the hell? Why would he do that...?

Although, the thought of Rhys priming himself prior to this was unexpectedly arousing. So that's what this fluffy feeling was. Oh, and that's why it was so difficult to concentrate on anything...?

"I was a little worried you might lose patience and not let me go through with it if it took too long. This way we can get straight to the good part." Rhys moved his finger around in there. "It's probably fine."

The hell it was! Julian could feel it was wet and throbbing, but he wasn't emotionally ready yet!

"Ah—!" There was a brief moment of panic, but when Rhys moved up to kiss him, it melted away.

So soft. It was like all the cells in his body were vibrating, making him feel mellow and relaxed.

All this time he'd been worried about Rhys moving too quickly, but as he lay there under the man, Julian's body was responding readily to the pleasure like he wanted to let go and surrender, like he needed something he couldn't quite describe.

Rhys shoved his dick in. It was rough and unceremonious, but it felt *good* in this state of arousal. Like the boundless space they lay in, Julian's insides gave way to the master of this realm. All of it was Rhys's, to do whatever he wished. What a blessing that he hadn't had to deal with the nerves for any longer or he might have missed out on how marvellous this felt.

"Ahhh, I see what you did, you sneaky bastard." Julian reached up to pull Rhys closer. "I love you."

"Goooooooood, aaah," Rhys thrust himself deeper, "because I love you so much it hurtssss... Aaaahhhh!"

CHAPTER 10

Vincent sat in a large tub of water. As the only person with any celebrity status on the island, they had twisted his arm until he'd given in. Several people had gathered around the game stand and given it a go, but it wasn't until Arthur hit the mark that Vincent fell into the tub.

"I'm sorry, brother, but someone had to do it." Arthur laughed heartily.

With how much worry Vincent had caused him and his whole family over the years, it seemed only fair. However, the water was ice-cold Arctic sea water, and while it wasn't as cold as in the winter, falling into it up to his waist was enough of a shock to bring back unpleasant memories. At least the cold got his mind off of Aurora, even if it meant he was now on the verge of panic.

The feeling lingered minutes later, even once he'd climbed out of the tub.

"Vincent!" It was Aurora's voice amidst the ringing in his ears. He turned to see her rush over. "Your knee! Did you hurt yourself?"

"No?" The knee. Right. It was fine, but the mention of it triggered more memories. It was a sunny day, but his wet trousers clung to his skin. It felt like torture. A severed finger rolling back and forth on the deck.

The partially decomposed corpse that had washed up on the shore lying motionless on the coroner's table. "I'm fine. I'm fine."

He forced himself to smile at Arthur and the rest of the crowd. They were only expecting some light-hearted fun. He wasn't supposed to ruin this for them, or else, what was the point of volunteering?

"I need to change out of these clothes..." Vincent stared at his legs. At least this didn't smell as bad. It was just water. But he couldn't breathe for fear it might still smell. They were all staring at him as if they already knew.

"Mother should have a dry set of clothes for you at the stall." Arthur had walked over to him. "I forgot about the knee. It was fine, though, right? You wouldn't have agreed to it, if it was hurting, right?"

"It's fine." There was no space left for anything but fine. Damage control. Keep it together. Everything was fine. This wasn't the first time, and it would pass.

"I'll help you." Aurora took Vincent by the hand and started leading him towards the stall where Aster and Celandine were selling their potpourri pouches and baked goods.

It would be better once his legs were no longer bound and weighed down by the wet trousers. He peeled them off in a daze but felt much better putting on the dry ones.

"You look a little pale, luv. Is something amiss?" Aster asked.

"I'm fine. Fine." It would be truthful in just a moment. He was almost sure of it.

"Vincent, hurry up! We're about to start judging the beverages." Like a hawk, the governor charged from between the stalls.

"Right. All right. Thank you." Vincent got up and staggered after the man. The knee was stinging somewhat and his limbs felt stiff, perhaps from the cold. They would warm up soon. He just needed to walk it off and keep walking.

"Did he seem all right to you?" Aurora wanted to run after Vincent and stop him, but he'd said he was fine. He didn't look fine, though.

"Hmm, I didn't notice anything, did you?" Mrs Bramble asked her sister.

"He seemed like his usual absent-minded self to me. I pray he doesn't catch a cold from getting wet, the way he always does, but it's a warm day, and we got him some dry clothes. It should be fine." Celandine was busy restocking her bun trays.

"He's like that sometimes. Disappears into his own world. You get used to it." Mrs Bramble squeezed and folded the wet trousers and spread them out to dry.

No, there was something off about Vincent, but Aurora couldn't quite figure out what it was. She'd seen her share of people coming out of night-mares in spells of hysteria and panic, and that had seemed similar, no matter how many times he'd said he was fine. In fact, his repetitive insistence was the most suspicious symptom. He'd been commendably forthright about his struggles thus far, even if Ren sometimes had to coax him to open up.

"I'm going to go see..." Aurora forgot to fill in an excuse. She headed over to the judging tent.

Vincent seemed to be settling into his judging duties without any out-ward problems. He was conversing with the people around him, acting normal. Maybe it was indeed her suffering from an overactive imagination?

Aurora watched him for a while to be sure, but when he didn't seem to be in distress anymore, she left him at it.

For the first time today, Vincent appreciated the distraction of having to put on his social mask and interact with the islanders.

"Hey, Vincent! How is Ren? And that doctor of yours?"

"Oh, my wife was asking for another set of those cups you threw for her. The cat has dropped a few, so we are running low."

"We are hosting a small get-together with a few of our friends for my husband's sixtieth birthday. Can you make it? We'd love for you to come!"

His hard work of paying more attention to them was bearing fruit. Regardless of wanting to see him dunked into a tub of water, they seemed to be chatting with him more like one of them than a celebrity visitor. They were also more likely to give him a hug in passing instead of gawking and putting him up on an undeserved pedestal.

The competitors were shamelessly trying to butter him up with gifts and compliments when he was making rounds with the rest of the judges, but it seemed to be an accepted part of the competition.

"What do we have this year, Charles?" The governor picked up a sample cup of mead and offered another to Vincent.

It had a hearty mouthfeel, but the sweetness of the honey did not overpower the subtle floral notes, so it left a pleasant, clean aftertaste.

"Hmmm, I see..." The governor gave a good show of tasting it, stretching out his cup for another pour, and taking his time before announcing it was not bad. "What do you think?" he asked Vincent.

Charles was refilling Vincent's cup before he could put it down. It tasted no less pleasant the second time.

"I think I'll need to taste the others to know for sure." Vincent lowered his cup when Charles wasn't looking to avoid it getting filled again and scribbled some notes on the piece of paper he'd been provided.

"Ah, wise words!" The governor patted his back and moved on to the next contestant.

There were eight contestants in total and each of them tried to squeeze as many refills as possible, so by the time Vincent was through, he'd forgotten all about his unpleasant dunking experience and enjoyed an enthusiastic conversation about the entries with the other judges in the privacy of the judging tent.

The competition was tight, and there was some debate between two of the candidates, which required some more sampling, bribery and heated words between the judges. However, the winner was eventually decided and sealed into an envelope to be revealed later in a prize ceremony.

The judges cleansed their palates with a cup of water and moved on to the ales, with the procedure following a similar pattern.

With so many hours between the pie contest and this current event, Vincent realised that he'd gone into this with more or less an empty stomach. He made an attempt to remedy the situation by gnawing on a cinnamon bun he'd received as a bribe.

The round of ales was tasty, but if he'd managed through the mead without getting as carried away as some of the other judges, the hops were doing more of a number on him now. Thankfully the cups were small when they were this plenty.

"We have the wines next. You're still free, aren't you?" The governor turned to Vincent after a budding skirmish had been settled between two of the other judges by offering them each refills until they could reach a consensus under the table.

"Yes, I suppose." Vincent glanced at Mr Jawbutte and Mr Dwindleby under the table with some concern as they were still continuing their tasting even after the result of the round had been sealed into its envelope.

"Good man." The governor suppressed a burp and tried to disguise it as him clearing his throat. "I'm afraid we may need a couple more fresh judges. Some of these young ones don't yet know how to pace themselves to give consistent ratings."

"It would seem so." Vincent nibbled on his bun, feeling some likely unwarranted optimism in his own ability to resume with the task.

"I'll be right back." The governor raised his voice to let everyone in the tent know there would be a five-minute pause before the judging continued and then excused himself.

Vincent sat down to rest his knee. What a rough day this was turning out to be.

"Vincent!" A familiar voice interrupted Vincent's efforts to sober up.

"James!" Vincent replied and took a sip of the water he'd been offered by one of the more sensible ladies overseeing the practicalities of the competition.

"How are you? I haven't seen you in a while!" The good doctor's moustache and beard had thrived since they'd last seen each other. They were only a smidge short of the size of a full-grown beaver.

"I took your advice and spent the winter on the mainland. We got back a few months ago, but I've been busy. I'm doing much better. How are you? How's the family?"

"I heard! Everyone's been saying how much happier you seem these days. Could it be the influence of a certain beautiful lady? I thought I saw you arrive with one today. When will you introduce her to us?"

"Oh, yes, she's..." Vincent tried to see whether Aurora was anywhere close by. She'd been by Aster and Celandine's tent a while ago. "She was there a minute ago. I'll come visit with her sometime if you'd like."

"That would be splendid! Are you still chatting with that cat of yours?" James winked as if referring to an inside joke.

"Swifty is doing fine, as well." Vincent dodged the meat of the question with his usual ease.

"Ah, sorry to interrupt." It was Edward. "We're about to start the next round."

"Oh? Right." Vincent drank the rest of his water.

"Is this your first time judging?" Edward seemed worried.

"Yes."

"I thought I would skip this year, but the governor caught me as I was heading to see my wife performing with the dancers. It's a good thing I knew to anticipate this. Did you prepare...?"

"Uh?"

"Please tell me you prepared yourself for this."

"What do you mean?" How was he supposed to prepare? Even if he'd realised he needed to prepare somehow, he'd been too busy to even consider it.

"Here." Edward offered him another glass of water. "This is the wine round. It's the most prestigious award. It's going to cause the most commotion and the most hassle. Do not accept any extra refills! Hold your cup from the top at all times, like this." He demonstrated with his own cup.

"All right." It didn't seem like it could get that much more difficult than the first two rounds.

"Did you eat before you came?"

"No..."

"Do you have something to eat?"

Vincent lifted the rest of his cinnamon bun.

Edward shook his head in apparent exasperation.

"I guess that's something. I'll try my best to keep them off your back, but you need to refuse those refills from the start or else they will each try to force one in."

Vincent hadn't realised it was going to be such a technical challenge, but how bad could it be? He was feeling fine. It was just a little wine and the cups were small.

True to Edward's warning, the next round dragged on for over an hour. Vincent managed to dodge the refills for a full forty minutes of it, but the last half an hour or so were a complete freight train collision inside the Great Grymswich tunnel: it got dark and violent, if only figuratively.

There were some very thinly veiled, elaborate insults being dished out about the other competitors in the most reprehensible lack of sportsmanship Vincent had ever seen.

Edward did a decent job of shielding him from the worst of it by acting as cannon fodder, but even he couldn't deter the most determined contestants.

"A thirty-minute recess!" The governor declared and sat down to digest. A few more judges had joined Mr Jawbutte and Mr Dwindleby under the table, and they were holding their own private event with some boisterous singing and laughter.

"That is simply unacceptable." The governor made no effort to disguise his distaste. The rest of the judges were seated nearby in various leaning angles, enjoying the fresh air and cold water as if trophies won through grave hardship.

Vincent sat back and sighed. He was drunk, but it didn't quite seem to hit the same way. He wasn't tired at all. He felt a little light-headed but fine.

Edward brought him a glass of water and a cheese roll, despite having faced near annihilation during round three.

"I'd better go find my wife and hide until the last round is done, or I'll be nursing my head tomorrow. I suggest you do the same." He hobbled off before the governor woke up from his stupor and could detain him.

It was probably some really very reasonably solid and sound advice, Vincent thought. But he wasn't feeling particularly *bad*, and there was only one more round left. With over half of the judges incapacitated, it would have been rude to withdraw when he was not nearly in as bad a shape as some of them.

At the half-hour mark, with most of the judges still a little too shaky to continue, the governor issued another twenty minutes of break time. It gave Vincent a chance to chat with James and some of his family members who had come to root for another extended family member taking part in the next round.

"It was so lovely to have you over for Midwinter before last. Did you enjoy yourself? Would you like some cake?" They were shamelessly taking advantage of the perceived close relationship James had with Vincent and started with the bribes, flattery and taste tests way before the round had even started. "Here's just a tiny taste of our famous buckthorn liquor. Please have some!"

As soon as the cup had been deposited into his hand and he'd made the mistake of politely raising it to his lips, Vincent was surrounded by the other competitors waiting to do the same.

"I'm sure we will start judging soon..." Vincent turned to the governor for clarification, but it seemed the man had fallen asleep in his chair. Someone would probably wake him up shortly. There was still time before the announced starting time, though.

Vincent took the tiniest, politest of sips from the offered cups and tried to catch whatever hints of flavours they supposedly carried. He had the foresight to make some notes, guessing that the longer this took, the less likely he was to remember what the different tastes were, and he wasn't keen on having to taste them again to be reminded.

"Vincent!"

"Huh? Yes?" He turned around to both Ren and Jasmine at the open end of the tent. Since this wasn't the best place for two young ladies to visit, he gathered up some concentration and headed over to meet them.

"We're leaving after the choir performance. Aunt Celandine has promised we can stay up late if you approve, and she suggested we do it at the back garden of the townhouse. Is that fine with you?"

"Yes, that sounds fine."

"Are you all right here? Aunt Aster wanted me to ask if you've remembered to eat any supper."

"I'll be done here soon, so I'll eat something after." With a belly full of drink, Vincent rubbed the bridge of his nose to call on his remaining senses.

"That's good. I'll tell Aunt Aster. I think she's brought some sandwiches. Don't stay too long, all right?"

"Ah, yes. Have you seen Aurora?"

"She's helping some of the dancers behind the stage after Mrs Dwindleby had to take her husband home just now."

"Oh, right." It seemed the underside of the table had lost at least one man without Vincent realising. "I'll find her once I'm done here. You girls have a good night. Don't stay up on my account. I might like to sit and watch the sun not setting with her."

Ren grinned. Vincent wasn't sure what he'd just said to warrant that response. Even Jasmine looked like she might want to giggle.

"Don't drink too much, or you'll miss it," Ren reminded him most sagely.

"I'm merely taste-tasting for the competition."

"Yes, and I've seen the state in which some of the judges leave this tent." She laughed. "They had to carry Mr Dwindleby."

"Right. I'll try to be careful. Oh." Vincent noticed the governor waking up and making some noise to question why no one had woken him up any earlier. "I think I need to get back to it so we can get this over with."

"Good luck!" Ren gave him a quick kiss on the cheek and ran off with Jasmine, giggling. He wasn't sure what was so funny but hadn't much time to worry about it when he was being called back into the tent.

Good luck, indeed. He braced himself. He needed to be more careful if he wanted to spend the rest of the evening with Aurora.

Oh dear, thought Aster Bramble at the sight of Vincent exiting the competition tent.

"That does not look good." She nudged her sister, who turned to look.

"He is mostly upright, which is more than what can be said about Mr Dwindleby, Mr Jawbutte and Mrs Foxglove." Celandine put away her crocheting and left the stall to go help Vincent find his way.

"Hello!" Vincent called out to Aster a little louder than necessary. He looked to be in good spirits when he staggered over. "I was told you had sandwiches?"

"Yes, we do indeed." Aster reached into her basket for a few. She also poured him a glass of water.

"I was not expecting it to take so long." He bit into the sandwich with the wanton hunger of someone who should have eaten hours ago.

"It's a disgraceful event, is what it is." Celandine huffed and returned to her crocheting.

"Let the men have their fun. It's only once a year they make such a spectacle out of it." Aster gave Vincent an encouraging smile. "I know it's maybe not the most sophisticated gathering, but I'm glad you decided to finally take part."

He'd been very stand-offish about participating in the Festival, so it was a nice surprise to see him come out of his shell enough to join them. It seemed Aurora might have been a positive influence after all.

"This is a good sandwich. Thank you!"

"There's no need to make a number. I can hear you just fine," Celandine muttered.

She seemed to be peeved about Aurora, still, and vented some of it by being curt. The girl had been nothing but courteous and good natured throughout their stay, so there really was no need for it, but Celandine had always been stubborn.

"Have you seen Aurora?" Vincent asked between bites.

"It's best you not bother her right now, the way you are." Celandine was being surprisingly protective considering her supposed animosity. Aster laughed at both her sister and Vincent's confused expression.

"She's right over there. She seems to be heading down to the beach." Aster pointed at the easily spotted red hair at the other end of the market square.

Vincent wolfed the rest of the sandwich, gulped down the water, got up and tripped on his feet. He had enough of his senses left to not end up eating dirt as dessert, but a landing might have looked less precarious than the funny jig he did to regain his balance.

"Don't forget your cane!" Aster reminded him.

"Ah, screw the cane." He stumbled but kept on walking. Thankfully he didn't seem to be as boisterous as the others, so while Aurora would have her hands full with him, he probably would not cause her any serious trouble.

Perhaps this would give him some courage to deepen their relationship, since it looked like he might be even a touch too polite and reserved, seeing how tediously slowly they had progressed the past few months. At this rate, they might really miss their chance of appeasing Celandine with some grandchildren.

Aster chuckled to herself. Well, if that happened, Celandine would just have to live with herself for not being more cooperative.

CHAPTER 11

I t was getting late, but the sun was nowhere near setting. Aurora abandoned the bustle of the Festival to catch a moment to herself on a rocky beach by the docks. There was a single seemingly disused boat shed at the far side, with a long but sturdy pier stretching out from the front.

She sat up on the side of the pier to watch the waves hit the white tops of the skerries somewhere afar. The smell of the sea was strong here. It wasn't the usual stuffy stench of algae, fish guts and bird excrement from the docks but more of a fresh, salty scent.

"Here you are." Vincent's words brought along a whiff of wine to mix with the sea breeze. Aurora turned to look.

"Did the judging finally end?"

"Yes, we got through everything." Judging by the clear but sluggish cadence of his speech and his unstable gait, he'd had a few too many this evening, yet he managed to totter to the pier and sit down without a mishap. "And I mean *everything*." He took a deep breath and fell to his back.

"Did you hit your head?" She'd heard a suspicious thunk.

"Yes." He chuckled. "I hope that knocked some sense into me. I should have known better than to accept any of their demands."

"Indeed. You've been busy all day. We've hardly seen each other." Aurora set her hand on his and watched him lay there peacefully.

"I missed you." He turned his hand around to grab hers. "I spent the last four hours going through the ales, the meads, the wines and the spirits to rank them in the right order, and I had no idea it was such an arduous, important task that some of them had to be tasted not just twice or thrice." He seemed to be making a great effort to not slur his words.

"That does sound troublesome." Aurora leaned in closer. "How do we get you home in that state?"

"I got here, didn't I? I'll be fine in a bit. I just need a little lie-down." After a moment, his eyes opened and he scrambled back up to sit. "Unless you wanted—? Did you want to?"

"Don't worry. I'm not in a hurry to go home yet. It's nice here with no one around."

"Oh, right." His cadence returned to its leisurely drawl, and he stared at the skerries for a while, then squeezed her hand. "This is fairly romantic, isn't it?"

"Yes. It is beautiful here."

The sun was low down enough to paint the sky a lovely range of pastel hues, and while the air was getting cool, she was wearing her cardigan, and his hand was warm in hers. It was one of those rare moments that trumped spending the evening poring through her research.

Vincent interrupted her quiet appreciation by toppling on top of her. He hovered there for a moment before kissing her, his mouth heated and spicy from the drinks.

He could have stood to be more graceful, but it didn't feel or taste unpleasant, just unexpected. Aurora let herself enjoy it for a while.

"Ah, we'd better stop." She pushed him off to force him to let go of her lips.

"What, why?" He opened his eyes and looked utterly heartbroken.

"Someone could walk in on us, and you're quite drunk."

"I'm sorry..." He made no move to sit aside. "Did you not like it? Was I not supposed to?"

"I liked it, but the timing..."

"It's never a good time," he grumbled. "Can't I? One more?" He leaned closer but stopped to wait just short.

"One more, but—"

He was already at it. It was tempting to let him, but they were out in the open, and, while most people would enjoy the Festival for a few more hours, there was no guarantee someone wouldn't have the same idea about taking a breather as they had.

"Vincent, no..."

"A little more?"

"No."

He looked like he might really start to cry.

"How about inside the boat shed?" he suggested. Aurora gave him a pointed look. "No? Ah, I guessed it might be a no..." He finally retreated back to sit. Aurora sat up, as well.

"Well, maybe." She'd been looking forward to it herself but was beginning to think there was never going to be a great time or the right place. Perhaps this would be a good way to start? It would leave plenty of room for improvement and a lot of reason to keep practising... She blushed.

"Really?" He yanked her up by the hand before she could say anything more.

She was pulled into the boat shed by a drunken lunatic, who pushed her against the wall by attacking her with his sloppy kisses. Her lunatic. She grabbed him by the hair on his neck and pulled him closer to give him a lesson on surprise attacks. He seemed to be losing his senses, inebriated and egged on by her like this. The breeze took a hold of the front door and slammed it shut.

The shed became dim.

Vincent made a sound like he'd choked or bitten his tongue and backed off abruptly. It took a moment for Aurora's eyes to adjust to the relative darkness, even though plenty of light was let in through the cracks near the bottom of the wall boards.

There was just the sound of water beneath the boat shed, and Vincent's ragged breaths.

"What's wrong?"

It was that look from earlier today.

"I'm fine. I—" He looked out of it, but his struggle to steady his breathing was more obvious because he was drunk.

"Did it frighten you? The door slamming."

Was he skittish merely because of the noise or because of something that happened last Midwinter? Or earlier, when he'd been roughed up in Grovestead? In any case, he no longer seemed at all in the mood to continue, so it must have been no small scare.

"N-no. It's nothing. I just—" He stepped back to the door to get some fresh air.

"Are you sure? You don't look fine. Can I help?" Aurora joined him. He was still breathing abnormally.

"I'm just drunk," he mumbled. She tried to take him by the hand, but he refused. "I need a moment..." He limped back out to the pier and thankfully sat down before he fell over the side. Aurora followed him.

"Do you want to talk about it?"

"No." His hands were shaking.

It reminded her of the time in her office after Hosta had yelled at him, but why would a slam trigger the same response? It was similar but not the same. He seemed irritated and rubbed his knee.

"That's too rough." She stopped him from mishandling himself. "You don't have to tell me, but I might be able to help if you do."

Vincent looked at her, massaged his frown, instead, and sighed.

"I appreciate that, but this will pass in a bit."

How sad that he wasn't comfortable enough to share, but it probably meant it was that difficult for him. No matter how curious Aurora was, she didn't think it was right to force it out of him.

"All right. Well, at least let me hold your hand until it does?" She offered it to him.

"I don't deserve that. I'm... damaged. I'm filthy," he whispered.

"Don't say that." Aurora took his hand and made him look up at her. "It's not true, but I wouldn't care if it were. You don't have to be perfect for me to love you."

"I'm sorry. I've had much too much to drink. I shouldn't have come here. I should—" He moved to get up.

"Don't go. Just relax. Stay there until you calm down and feel better. I'll shut up if you want some quiet."

"Ah, I..." He hesitated. "Well, I can't go now, can I?" He was still holding on to his promise literally.

She smiled and gave him a hug, but for whatever reason this seemed to make him even more unhappy, and he recoiled only further.

"Can't you please just tell me?" she implored him, now at a loss for what else she could do that wouldn't just end up making it worse. "It's killing me to see you like this!"

"I-I suppose... I could try." He looked tortured. "But my head is not at its best. I'll probably end up explaining it all wrong. You'll think I'm no good..."

"You know I wouldn't. Surely, you must know that, right?" She squeezed his hand. It was still shaking.

"I know, I just— I don't— I—"

"Does it have something to do with the knee?" Aurora had long since guessed a lot of that pain was mental. How had he injured it originally? What on earth had happened to him?

"Yes." He stopped rubbing it. "I messed up."

Aurora said nothing. He seemed to be working up to it.

"I really shouldn't have tried to weasel out of my responsibilities, but that's what I've done all my life," he added after several minutes of silence. He sounded deceptively close to sober now. "I was supposed to write my book. I promised I would, but I didn't take it seriously. It was a nuisance. I never should have promised to do it in the first place."

Aurora waited.

"The editor they assigned to me, he was much too young. He tricked me into staying for the winter, the winter before last. He didn't know any better. I let it happen.

"All he wanted was for me to write, and I let him down in so many ways it messed him up. Yes, sure, I didn't make him do it, but I also never made an effort to understand or be there for him. He was so young."

"Make him do what?"

"He beat me up when I was raving mad from hypothermia and locked me into a cellar for... I'm not sure how long."

"He what?!" Aurora had expected something, but it wasn't this.

"I drove him into a corner, so he jumped off the snowtrain. I jumped after to save him. I was sick as usual at the time, so after I eventually succumbed to the cold, he must have dragged me to the cabin at the cape. I was mad with rage when he was forced to defend himself and struck at me.

I don't remember it very well, but I think that was when I busted the knee. Then he locked me into the earth cellar."

"Excuse me, he what? He didn't take you to the doctor first thing?"

"No, he was afraid I would turn him in. It was all probably in self-defence or an accident, but I was not in my right mind, and he must have sensed it."

"How long were you in there? How did you get out?" An earth cellar in the winter must have felt confined, cold and dark, which explained his reaction to the boat shed.

"I don't remember. There was no way to tell time. It happened after Midwinter... It might have been for weeks. He moved me up to the attic for a while, and that's when I finally got the bucket—" He buried his face into his hands.

Weeks. In a cold, dark cellar. Bucket? For what? Wait. Aurora grasped it.

"You lay there injured with no means to...? Without...?"

"Yes."

Aurora could not imagine what that must have been like.

"Ren inadvertently saved me by distracting Jones so I could get away, but I didn't know it at the time. Like a bloody fool, I crawled off in the worst possible direction, ended up wading onto the ice and jumped into the sea to avoid him. I wouldn't be here if George and Arthur hadn't fished me out in the nick of time."

"What happened to your editor?" It wasn't the most pressing question, but it was at the tip of her tongue.

"I'm not sure. I think he might have killed himself, but I don't know the details. All I remember is seeing his severed finger on deck when I was rescued. I don't know how it got there." He paused. "But if I'd paid more attention, if I'd been nicer to him, could I have stopped it from happening?"

"There's no way to know something like that for sure. But it's not your responsibility to save someone so troubled. I don't care if you refused to write the book entirely, there's no excuse to lock you up, especially when you were injured."

"He was right to defend himself, though. I jumped at him when I thought he'd burnt down my cottage, but as it turned out, it was my friend Edward." Vincent shook his head and sighed.

"Excuse me?" Aurora had heard that the cottage had had to be rebuilt after a fire, but it had been intentional? What sort of a 'friend' was this Edward?

"He meant to destroy some files in my basement while I was sleeping, but he accidentally ended up burning the place. At least I managed to save Swifty."

"You were in there?!"

That look he'd had at the ReM Clinic when he'd looked up through the skylight at Aurora and mentioned the cat... When he'd been dunked into the cold water today... When he'd been shut in the boat shed just now... How many times had he relived these experiences? How many were there? Surely this was excessive for one person to bear.

"Yes. I should have known better than to pin it on Jones, but in my defence, I was severely sleep deprived." He chuckled, trying to make light of it. "Edward was doing it because Aster asked him to. They were all just worried about me. I shouldn't make everyone so worried about me." The way he was smiling when he looked at Aurora was more painful than a thousand daggers.

"Please, Vincent..." She hugged him tight. "Please stop..."

"I'm sorry. I know, I'm hopeless."

"That's not what I meant!" Aurora let go of him to look him in the eyes and make sure he was listening properly. "I want you to stop assuming responsibility for everything! Please stop blaming yourself for other people's mistakes! Aren't you reading my thoughts? Why aren't you picking this up?!"

Vincent looked shaken.

"I'm sorry! I wasn't paying attention! I'm... I'm not at my best... It's been a long day and, honestly, I really should have told the governor no after the first two competitions..." He leaned his head on Aurora's shoulder and heaved a sigh. "I'm sorry."

"Don't be. It's the world that owes you an apology."

"If you're not mad at me, the world owes me nothing."

For someone supposedly hopeless and drunk, he sure knew the thing to say to tug at Aurora's already taut heartstrings. She sighed and rubbed his back.

"Am I right in assuming you haven't told this to anyone?" she asked.

"Why would I advertise that I sat in my shit for weeks and rolled into the sea to escape it like an idiot?" He did not lift his head from her shoulder when he said it.

"They're all assuming you're fine when you're not. You could have told them an abridged version, at least, to stop them from roping you into things that are clearly traumatic for you, like dipping you into ice-cold water for laughs."

"They just wanted some harmless fun, and I didn't fully realise it myself until I was already in it."

"Well, I would have stopped you had I known! For the sake of your knee, as well. Does it still hurt? I'm sorry I can't give you something for it because you've been drinking."

"It's not so bad now. I feel better," he said, but he had to curve his tall frame quite a lot to lean on Aurora's shoulder, and he'd even slid lower down somewhat. It looked far from comfortable.

"It really is fine. You don't have to worry about me," he mumbled into the front of her dress.

So now you're listening in?

"Yes."

You're truly feeling better?

"Yes. Thank you."

Would you like to resume what we were doing if we put a rock between the door so it doesn't slam shut?

Aurora waited. Vincent snuggled against her, with his cheek practically on her breast.

"Yes." He looked up at her. "You said that, right? I'm not just imagining things because I'm drunk?"

"If you're up for it."

"I'm definitely up for it. Please lead the way." A little unsteady on his feet, Vincent followed Aurora with surprising speed and accuracy. "I'm sorry, I might be a bit clumsy." He slammed the door shut behind them and jumped at her.

"Oh, ah... Really?"

He certainly didn't seem clumsy when he unclasped her corset, buried his face in her bosom and unbuttoned the few buttons of her chemisette with his teeth.

"I'll make it up to you later. I'll be a gentleman. I'll do all the things you need, but right now, forgive me for rushing..."

And that was her dress skirt, petticoat and even her drawers pulled down and kicked aside as swiftly as nothing. She barely had time to notice from his heated kisses and warm hands caressing her body as he stripped off her layers.

Vincent lay her down on the pile of clothes and relieved her of the chemisette to kiss her breasts. He seemed busy with that, so she reached to open the front of his trousers. When she slid her hand along the length, he almost fell on top of her.

"A— hmm, ah, Aurora... What are you—?"

"Did you think I would just lie down and wait for you to finish? Here..." She guided his other hand to her breast. "I need you to concentrate. Do the thing you just did, but use your tongue and do it here."

He did as told but flinched and almost bit her nipple when she held Gerard to get reacquainted with its girth and extent.

"Oh Guardian, Aurora, my love, what are you doing to me? Ahh..." He looked at her with his eyes losing focus.

"Don't stop what you were doing." She used her other hand to warm herself because it seemed Vincent wasn't going to have the attention span to put much else but his mouth to good use.

"I'm sorry, I—"

"I don't mind. Your mouth is plenty enough." Especially when she tugged him just right and made him interrupt himself with some deep and delicious grunting noises while trying to suck her nipple.

"Love, please..." He let go of the nipple. "You told me to concentrate, but I'm afraid I can only concentrate on what you're doing."

"A little more, and I'm ready." She pulled him closer and kissed his gorgeous face. His penis was pressed against her, and its firmness felt encouraging. He looked eager and wanting, but there was a hint of that low self-esteem insecurity visible on his face as he struggled to know what to do.

"I'm sor—"

Before he could finish another apology, Aurora pushed him aside with all her strength. It was surprisingly easy with his current poor sense of balance, and he looked thoroughly confused when she climbed on top of him and sat on Gerard.

"I'll do it. Don't worry." She adjusted him to where he could easily slide inside.

"Uhhh?" His eyebrows were like a poorly constructed fur suspension bridge swaying in the wind as he searched for his concentration in vain.

Aurora lifted her pelvis to test how it would feel. He grabbed her waist and self-indulgently pulled her back down.

"Let me do it," she reminded him.

"Ah, sor— ahh…"

By searching for the best position, she stopped him from yet another apology. He seemed to be responding favourably to her experiments, and with a few more tries, she found the perfect pace and angle.

Ah, yes, that was it. That was how she remembered it. Oh, Gerard! It made her insides turn into soufflé with each thrust. She wanted to be absolutely ruined by it, and he obliged by pushing her up with each thrust.

"Aurora— please— uh—"

"Wh— at—?"

"Can— you, ah— not—"

"Huh? Ahh—"

"Call— that— name?"

"Oh— ahh—" You're listening in on me?

"Yes—" He stopped moving. "Ah, should I stop?"

Aurora paused to catch her breath.

"No, no. Was it distracting? I'm sorry, I couldn't help myself." Her obliterated soufflé was throbbing and pleading for this guardianbysmal intermission to stop, but she didn't want to make it uncomfortable for him.

"Soufflé?" Vincent frowned.

"It feels warm and fluffy…" Aurora blushed. Vincent's frown turned into a smile.

"I should have known Gerard was a hungry glutton." He gave her another push.

Her knees and thighs turned into pudding. When he set the pace, she lost her capacity for thought and hadn't even the sense to kiss him to stop herself from moaning.

"Vin— cent— ah— n— cent—"

...Vincent, Vincent, Vincent, Vincent...

Vincent closed his eyes.

...Vincent, Vincent, Vincent, Vincent...

His eyebrows tightened to such a deep furrow, they formed an impregnable thicket fence.

...Vincent, Vincent, Vincent, Vincent...

After a few more thrusts, the eyebrows tried to recalibrate but seemed to give up completely. He let out a noise and started to spasm as he pushed.

Aurora heard the deep satisfaction in his voice, and the sound made her follow suit in time to catch his last orgasmic pushes.

Vinnnceeeennntttt!

"Aaah," he gasped for breath and opened his eyes to watch her. She could still feel the shakes reverberating through her body.

"I love you." She slumped forward to kiss him, too weak and mellow to manage anything else.

"You've certainly dispelled all my doubts about it." He squeezed her. "I love you, too."

"Good." She smiled.

"I'll love you even more once I've sobered up. I'll love you until you're sick of me. I'll love you for as long as you'll let me."

The poor man was reduced to incomprehensible rambling, drunk from both the copious amounts of alcohol and his orgasm.

"That's a long time. You'd better...!" She lay on top of him.

"Or you won't forgive me?"

"At least for a week..." She wanted to cry.

"A week is too long." He squeezed her again. "I'd better make sure I love you all the way to oblivion."

Chapter 12

The idea had been brewing in Rhys's mind for a few months, but it was now taking a more tangible shape.

He'd gone to see Hosta at her new apartment in the Ear of the City to discuss some treatment options for Julian and possibly also for Vincent if the man happened to have a relapse. She'd offered Rhys some tea, apologised for a few more of her transgressions that she'd managed to recall and promised him her full cooperation.

"Have you uncovered anything useful?" Rhys asked.

"No, but I've been busy looking into this James I was married to. I found some worrying log entries on memory procedures done to me in recent years that I had not authorised. It leads me to believe he may have been erasing things I hadn't agreed to. I think that's the reason for my current state, but I'm slowly piecing it all together and sending Vera any data that could prove useful."

She explained she'd declared bankruptcy and shut down Hosta Therapy with the exception of some of the treatment centres that were doing reputable work in the field. She'd let them continue as their own unaffiliated entities.

Some of the less reputable contracts were causing her issues, but she'd hired a team of "specialists" to tackle them and seemed hopeful things would settle down soon. It sounded promising.

There was still one pressing question weighing on Rhys's mind, though.

"This is going to seem odd, but I'm hoping to throw Vincent a surprise birthday party. The problem is none of us know when his birthday is..."

"Oh? That's easy. It's the first of July. Come to think of it, that's exactly a week from now." She tasted her tea and frowned. "I've been sending Justin to see him this time of year to check how he's doing. Do you think Justin might do that for me again if you asked him? I don't actually have anything left to connect to him with. We lost everything in the fire. There might be a few units around, but... I suppose it's time for me to let him go?"

"I can ask him." A week was not a lot of time to throw a surprise birthday party, especially since Rhys was yet to even chat with Vincent about when they would see each other next. "But I don't think Vincent would mind it if you stopped by yourself, even if for just a few minutes. He didn't seem too upset with you last Midwinter."

"I know. That's what worries me. If he's anything like his father, I'd better not risk it."

"He's not at all like our father."

"Ah, I keep forgetting you're also Walter's child. My condolences."

"What about Julian?" Rhys asked.

"What about him?"

"When's his birthday? He said it's in April but couldn't recall the exact date."

"That troublesome child. We did not go as far as to remove each and every bit of his past! He should remember that much at least. I sent him cards, for Guardian's sake!"

"I know!" What an unexpected place to find kinship, but really, Rhys had wanted to vent about Julian's carelessness ever since he'd found out the man hadn't paid attention to such a simple thing. "I'm going to make him remember it next time!"

"Good! It's the sixteenth. If you have a big party, try to keep track of his drinking, all right?"

"I'll make sure he doesn't cause a scene. Don't worry. He's been doing well reining in his temper lately."

"Oh, that's not why I'm worried. Yes, he can get unruly when he drinks, but unless especially provoked, he's usually only nasty towards me when he's like that." Hosta paused and looked away for a moment. "Perhaps rightfully so." She exhaled heavily before turning back to Rhys. "But I'm more concerned for his health. He doesn't pay attention to his limits, drinks more than he should, and you saw how he gets when he randomly connects to his brother and remembers him. It's awful to watch."

Rhys felt like an idiot for assuming she was merely concerned about the safety of the onlookers. Why had it been so easy to believe it wasn't out of genuine concern for her son?

"I'll keep an eye on him," Rhys promised.

With the dates clear, his next move was to check whether it was possible to hold the party on Vincent's birthday or if he'd have to postpone it, and also, whether there was a way to incorporate Julian's birthday celebration into the mix, because, while Rhys had baked him a cake in April, it had tasted too bland to be the proper, memorable birthday cake he'd intended.

Rhys wanted a redo, and he didn't want to wait a full year for it.

He also wanted to bring Justin's remains along to Grovestead and ask whether Quin would be willing to host him at his estate and perhaps even dig out a small duck pond on the property for his amusement. Justin was Julian's twin, so persuading Quin didn't seem like it would pose much of a challenge.

A week wasn't a lot of time for the arrangements, but it didn't seem entirely impossible.

J ulian seemed to be having an off day after an unusually lengthy streak of decent days.

"You're going to go to Grovestead *right now*?"

"Yes. Vincent's birthday is in a week. I managed to get a hold of Vera, and she said it was a great idea to spend a week in Grovestead without the girls. It'll give them a chance to see how well Ren and Jasmine can manage on their own without Vincent hovering around, to find out if Ren is ready to go to that girls' school in Chattsmouth. My guess is she'll do fine, but it doesn't hurt to check whether she changes her mind about not wanting to separate from Vincent so soon."

"I'm busy with the inventory with all my orders arriving this week. I can't come with you."

"I realise that. And I know I said I'd help, but I didn't know Vincent's birthday was going to be next week. You understand, right? Victor can help you, yeah?" Rhys turned to Victor, who was washing his brushes in a bucket at the back of the back room where they were having this discussion.

Victor looked up from his brushes but said nothing. More importantly, he did not object.

"Grovestead is closer to Whitskersey, so less of a drive for Vincent and his family, and Quin said he doesn't mind hosting us. There's plenty of space. I'm going to invite everyone he knows who can make it on such short notice. We've even invited the Brambles with the excuse that they're heading to see relatives in Herring Cove tomorrow. The girls will be staying with someone called the Steadfasts while the Brambles are away. Vera said they have a girl of a similar age, and the father is an old friend of Vincent's, albeit he's coming to the party and leaving the girls to his wife to take care of."

In truth, there weren't as many people to invite on Vincent's behalf as there were for Julian. Even with the risk that Julian would find it intensely uncomfortable to meet the people from his past, it would be worth it to reintroduce him to his friends and the people in whose lives he had been a positive influence. He would survive a single evening of awkwardness, and it would be overall easier on him to not know about it in advance.

Luckily Quin had travelled ahead some days prior to take care of some unrelated business things, so he was already hard at work making the arrangements and getting in touch with their mutual acquaintances.

"You could have just told me you didn't want to do the inventory. No need to make up such elaborate excuses." Julian actually rolled his eyes.

"Some of us think birthdays are important and should be celebrated!" Rhys gave him a pointed look. "What's got you in such a crabby mood today, anyway? It's no more than a week. Maybe distance will make the heart grow fonder."

"Perhaps."

If Julian's eyes had been as sharp as they looked, he could have stabbed someone to death with them, regardless of their outwardly harmless spherical shape.

"You'll still come to Grovestead on the first, though, right? You wouldn't miss your brother's birthday party because of some stupid inventory?"

"I don't know how long it's going to take. Now, if you'll excuse me, I think I have a customer waiting." Julian marched out of the room to seethe at the poor thing.

Victor wrapped his brushes with a cloth to squeeze them dry.

"I'll make sure we're done in time," he said.

"Good. I hope he's not this crabby all week." Rhys reached up to pat Victor's shoulder.

"I don't mind." Victor fidgeted with his beard. There was a hint of a smile he was trying to hide.

"Have fun, Victor." Rhys chuckled.

"Oh. Oh, I think I will." He collected his brushes and supplies and headed back upstairs.

"Tell me how it went, later, all right? I want to hear!" Rhys yelled after him.

While Julian was out to arrange some of the larger deliveries, Victor manned the till in his stead. A stocky, somewhat unkempt gentleman walked in, took off his hat and clutched his cane. It had been raining outside, so he was a bit of a sorry sight.

"Evening, sir," Victor forced himself to say.

"Good evening." The man walked up to the counter. "Is Mr Wakefield in today?"

"No, I'm afraid not, sir."

"Who are you? What happened to the unpleasant pharmacist?"

"He is also currently out. How may I help you, sir?"

"Ah, guardemn it." The man leaned on the counter in an unexpected show of raw frustration. "There really is no way of buying the place, is there?"

Ah, right. This was Mr Ballroth. He had come around many enough times for Victor to have caught a glimpse of him on occasion.

"I'm afraid not, sir. We are happily occupied."

Mr Ballroth sighed heavily.

"May I suggest not wasting more of your time?" Victor felt bad for the man. Whatever was making him come back time and time again must have been important to him. He'd not even wanted to make a good deal with the purchase.

"I suppose…" He straightened himself, but he was at an age where straight was a forward-leaning angle. "Do you mind if I rest here for a moment before I head out there again?"

Since it was raining heavily, and there was no reason to deny his request, Victor gestured for him to take a seat at Rhys's former consultation corner.

The man ambled to the sofa and sat down with some difficulty. What was an apparently wealthy, old man like him going to do with a building like this? Wouldn't he rather have enjoyed retirement with the money he had?

Victor had no reason to pry, so he resumed taking inventory while there were no customers.

The rain was not letting up any, and the front room felt a touch chilly, so Victor climbed upstairs to make himself a cup of tea. Since the gentleman was still sitting on the sofa when he came back, he offered him the extra cup he'd made just in case.

Mr Ballroth thanked Victor and took the cup, clearly surprised by the hospitality. Victor returned to the inventory.

After a half an hour of silence and with no sign of the rain stopping, Mr Ballroth brought the empty teacup and saucer to the counter and gave another polite thanks.

"I will not bother you again," he said, wiped his nose into a handkerchief and put his hat back on. "But if Mr Wakefield ever decides to sell, you know where to find me."

"Yes, sir."

"Are you not going to ask?"

"Sir?"

"I've been coming here every month since you returned last year. Surely you're at least mildly curious?"

"It's none of my business, sir," Victor said. Because the man looked so disappointed, he added, "but I would not mind knowing."

Mr Ballroth looked relieved. He took his hat back off and started recounting. Once he was done, he thanked Victor again and hobbled over to the door.

"Please help yourself to the umbrella to your left. It was left behind by the previous owner. It's old but it works, and there's no need to return it," Victor told him.

Mr Ballroth glanced at the umbrella hanging from a peg and took it with thanks before heading out the door.

CHAPTER 14

Julian arrived at the pharmacy just as the odious Mr Ballroth stepped out the door. Thankfully, the man said nothing when he passed because Julian was in no mood to deal with the likes of him.

"Did we have any actual customers?" Julian put away his umbrella and turned to Victor at the counter.

"No." Tight-lipped as ever.

"Must be the rain. I thought Mr Lumberthatch would have come to pick up his medication today." Julian set aside his hat, gloves and rain coat.

"There's still an hour," Victor reminded him. "I'll go make us supper."

Julian switched places with Victor and realised the man had already gone through the stock in one of the two large cabinets and started on the other. It took mere minutes to run out of things to do as the refills for the remaining empty drawers weren't to be delivered until the next day. Julian twiddled his thumbs in silence until quarter to closing time when, with the streets emptied by the now murky drizzle, he decided to close the shop.

The scent of supper greeted Julian at the stairs.

The wood burner crackled with warmth in the gentle light of the upstairs lounge. There were no candles or flowers on the dining table, but it was set with care, and the atmosphere said more than whatever words Victor could have forced out of his mouth.

Victor took notice of Julian the moment he came up the stairs. Julian had time and time again misinterpreted that furtive look as suspicion or mistrust, but its meaning was now unmistakably obvious, even to him.

"This seems elaborate."

The meal Victor was about to serve was not something he'd slapped together for mere sustenance. How long had he planned this? Had he assumed he'd get the chance eventually and planned for it just in case in the course of however many days? Or had he made these preparations in haste the moment he'd realised the others would be out of the house?

"Take a seat. I'm nearly done." The man filled the plates with what could easily rival a Midwinter feast.

Julian sat down feeling conflicted. He fingered the edge of a neatly folded napkin. The cutlery seemed unusually shiny. Everything on the plate was sliced and diced with such precision it must have taken a significant amount of time to prepare for someone unused to cooking. Victor had even garnished the dishes with fresh herbs.

"Would you like some wine?" the man offered. It looked to be something not from the downstairs larder.

"Ah, right. Yes, sure." How could he refuse when his host must have bought it especially for the occasion?

Victor's company had hardly ever felt awkward, but this did make Julian feel too self-conscious for comfort. What were Victor's expectations for this supper and could he even hope to meet them? The man had gone through so much trouble, too much trouble for just Julian's sake.

The slight tremor in his hand as he poured the wine was the only detail betraying Victor's nerves. He seemed remarkably calm for someone presenting a supper so romantic it should have ended with an ask for Julian's hand in marriage. He even gave Julian an embarrassed smile and a chuckle that didn't sound forced or rehearsed.

"It's not meant to be anything special. I just got a little carried away." Victor poured himself some wine, set the bottle aside and took his seat.

He seemed to have said it in earnest, but Julian had to wonder whether it was prudent to pretend this didn't mean something. Victor had only ever been considerate about his infatuation: he was keen to show it but tried hard not to make Julian feel uncomfortable as a consequence. Meanwhile, Julian routinely forgot the man was even there or within earshot the times he was busy with either Rhys or Quin.

"I am not worth this." These words had never rang truer than when they boomed in Julian's ears now. How inconsiderate was he? How self-absorbed? He felt like scum.

"Don't worry about it. I enjoyed making it."

And what other forms of self-torture do you routinely engage in to seek pleasure from pain? Am I to believe this is part of your character, and I'm not to worry about it? Julian thought. He couldn't shake off the clammy grip of guilt clutching at his throat as he tried to swallow a forkful of the generous feast prepared for him.

"Is it no good?" Victor sounded worried.

Julian choked, coughed and hit his chest to dislodge the offending piece.

"There's nothing wrong with it." It was truly a well-rounded, well-prepared meal, even if its intricacies were lost on Julian who didn't usually pay attention to such things. The fault lay solely in its subpar recipient.

Julian emptied his glass to wash down what was left in his mouth. What a waste of food and of perfectly good wine.

"You don't have to eat it if it's not to your liking. I won't take offence, don't worry." Victor refilled his glass.

"You should bloody well take offence!" With his fingers still clasped on the edge, Julian backed off from the table.

V ictor set down his knife and fork. Julian raising his voice might have caused him to flounder in the past, but even if it did make his pulse quicken by a fair number of beats, it wasn't out of fear or worry.

He was calm enough to hear the words from their raging volume, and while he was no mind reader, he could figure out the gist: Julian wasn't mad *at* him but rather *for* him. The man had avoided taking so much as an errant glance ever since he'd come up, yet Victor felt more seen than he had for a while.

Being seen was usually an unpleasant experience for him, but this time it felt distinctly good.

"Thank you."

Julian looked up from where he was hunched over, wrestling with his anger.

"You have nothing to feel bad about, but I appreciate it." Had it been too painful to handle, Victor would have left. By choosing to stay, he was equally responsible for whatever emotional damage they had inadvertently dealt him. And honestly, because the three of them were all dear to him, it didn't feel that bad to be neglected or ignored occasionally.

Julian was still staring at him, and evidently the unexpected thanks had been enough for him to forget his anger for the time being.

"If there's nothing wrong with it, you should eat it before it gets cold," Victor suggested and resumed his meal.

Julian pulled himself and his chair back to the table but looked hesitant.

"Don't worry about it," Victor added. It wasn't as if they were *all* continuously neglecting him. Quin had always been nothing but kind and inclusive.

Julian might not appreciate knowing all the details of that particular relationship, but knowing about them might be the thing to make him aware of his feelings if there were feelings there to be made aware of.

Maybe he needed a bit of a push? Maybe he needed to realise it didn't have to feel the same as with either Rhys or Quin. The man would have definitely turned Victor down if there was absolutely nothing there to build on. Or he would do so now, if put on the spot, and perhaps it was worth knowing for sure either way.

Julian ate, determined but failing to enjoy his meal. Perhaps it would have been easier had it tasted ghastly. He'd eaten food prepared more masterfully on occasion, but this had absolutely nothing wrong with it.

So why did it feel like he wasn't supposed to enjoy it?

"I'll make something less fancy tomorrow," Victor said.

"I'll cook."

"Take turns?" Victor signed.

"I'll do it. I'm used to doing it."

Victor didn't look pleased. He lifted his hands seemingly about to sign something but spoke up instead, "You can make the breakfast, but I'm cooking lunch, and you're welcome to eat it or cook something else for yourself, but I need the practice."

"Oh." Julian ran his fingers across his forehead in an attempt to smooth out its creases. Again, it would have been rude to refuse. He was sinking deeper into this debt he didn't know how to repay. "Why is it so damn delicious?" he blurted out, exasperated.

Victor had a suspicious, sheepish, even shifty, look to him.

"What? Why do you look so guilty?"

"I exchanged notes."

Didn't it look like Victor was stifling a laugh behind that damn beard of his? Was he amused or nervous? Which was it?

"What notes? Is there something in this?" Julian poked it with his fork and tried to recall whether it was something he'd ever expressed liking. "Quin! Damn it, you exchanged notes? With Quin?" That was cheating! Here he'd agonised over his guilt while Victor was being sneaky and serving him one of his unknown favourites! Argh, the nerve!

"That's why I said not to worry about it. I just didn't want to pick something you hate. Don't read too much into it."

"You could have asked *me!*"

"Well, Quin happened to be there and the subject came up. Besides, you don't pay attention to these things as much as he does..."

"So he's the more reliable expert?!" Julian banged his fists on the table.

"Watch out for the glass."

"When did you chat with Quin anyway? When did the two of you become best buddies?" Julian resisted the urge to re-pound the table.

Victor shrugged and, already finished with his supper, collected his plate and glass away and took them to the sink. "Once I got over the envy, it really didn't take much." There was definitely at least half of a grin hiding behind that beard, and it wasn't even remotely a spasm born from the nerves. "We have similar tastes, after all, and he's so darn willing to please... Are you done?"

Julian checked his plate and hurried to scoop the last of the tubers and sauce with his fork. When he was done, Victor cleared the table save for the refilled glass of wine. Again, the man had somehow managed to divert Julian's attention away from the anger, even if the underlying irritation was still there.

"I wish you didn't discuss things like that behind my back. You know how much I hate feeling like people know more about me than I do."

"Maybe you should spend more time chatting with Quin yourself, then, and stop avoiding the subject." Victor poured himself a digestif and retreated to one of the armchairs.

"That's what Rhys always tells me." Julian sighed. He watched the full wine glass with some lingering suspicion.

When he recalled the real reason why his mother had stood on guard every time he drank so much as a sip, that feeling of unease subsided. Yes, he'd likely done some horrendous things while drunk and struck with grief—especially when that grief had been fresh—but time had been a soothing friend. It hadn't taken away the pain completely, and his propensity to anger and shaky self-control were still there, but none of it was as frightening as the unknown.

Julian took the glass and joined Victor in the other armchair.

"What else did he tell you?" How curious that Quin had managed to wriggle himself into Victor's trusted, select group of friends he was willing to have a casual chat with. Maybe it shouldn't have been surprising considering Quin's sociable personality... "Hold up. What was it that you said about Quin?"

"Which part?" Victor rubbed his beard. "Hmm, I said I was over the envy, but can we not talk about him?"

What the hell was Quin scheming, buttering up Victor to make him think he was eager to please? Julian was curious and peeved but hadn't the heart to press after such a forthright request to change the subject. And if Victor was willing to make do with some friendly banter as thanks for the meal, it was only fair the man got to choose the topic. "What would you like—"

"Actually, let's talk about Quin."

"Huh?"

"He's too much of a pushover, and I'm sure he enjoys whatever attention you're willing to give him, but please stop being so rough on him!"

Julian blinked. "Now you really sound like Rhys—"

"It's not like he hates it if you're gentle with him. He's responsive either way."

"He's what?"

"Responsive. So unless you're a sadist, there shouldn't be a problem with treating him more kindly more often."

"Are you drunk? What are you talking about?" Julian stared at Victor in disbelief.

"Sex." Victor signed it as he said it. There was no mistaking it.

"W-what?" Julian glanced at his wine glass, but it was still full. There was no blaming that, so why had this conversation shifted to such surreal territory?

Somewhere at the back of Julian's mind, he remembered Quin saying he wouldn't mind 'entertaining that', so, was *that* what this was? Had they—? Why else would Victor know? Surely that wasn't a conversation people usually had... Although, wasn't this a similar conversation? So, perhaps to Victor, for whom all topics were equally difficult, sex was just a thing to discuss among many. And Quin seemed like he would strike up a conversation about anything, so—

"I assumed it was fine since you never objected when it was brought up, but I realise now I should have made sure... If it makes you uncomfortable, we won't do it again." Victor seemed serious.

"You had, you, when?" Well, trust Quin to seize any chance he got. That rat.

But hadn't he also seemed obsessed enough with Julian to not...? What was this deeply unsettled feeling? Not anger precisely, not so much betrayal... Disappointment? Jealousy? Was he this dependent on having someone adore him *exclusively?*

"It was that night when you were busy with Rhys. I thought you put two and two together when we busted through the door."

Crap. He'd been so preoccupied, he'd not given it a second thought! Indeed, there had been something peculiar happening there, and evidently, it hadn't been as simple as Victor catching Quin eavesdropping at the door.

"You really hadn't realised?" Victor frowned. "He was so torn over it, I was worried. I thought it would help to distract him."

"It was your idea?"

"I don't know whose idea it was, but I'm not precisely immune to everything. You may forget I'm around, but that doesn't mean I don't have ears."

"You're saying it was essentially my fault?"

"I don't think it was anyone's *fault*. I can't say I was hugely inconvenienced by it, and he seemed to enjoy himself on the whole. A little forewarning and communication would have been nice on your part, but I wouldn't consider it a bad evening."

From Julian's perspective, the evening had indeed been far from bad, so how could it feel so bad after the fact? He emptied his glass and set it aside to have it out of his hands should he be tempted to throw something later.

"Damn it, Quin," he mumbled.

"Don't be mad at him. He adores you. And you love him, don't you? So wouldn't you rather he enjoyed himself? Doesn't it make you feel a little less bad about prioritising Rhys sometimes?" Victor put his glass aside, leaned back and closed his eyes.

"Yes, but..." That all made sense, and Julian had been a hair away from thinking the same himself. But wasn't Quin always messing with him, trying to shove him out of balance somehow, on purpose? And if he wasn't mad at Quin, then what was this? Why did this feeling persist?

"What's there to sulk about?" Victor voiced the question.

"I don't know. I'm not sure..."

"Everyone loves and adores you. Aren't you happy?"

"Yes, but..." They weren't doing that exclusively, now, were they? Even Victor had—

Julian looked at Victor resting in the armchair with his eyes closed. The man reached back to remove the hair tie from his hair and tossed it to the side table.

He could be in plain sight and use more words than he usually used in a week, yet Julian would be too dense to understand he was there.

"I think I might turn in early, if you don't mind. We can probably finish your inventory and replenish your stock if we work hard tomorrow. Then, if we take the train the following morning, we'll make it to Grovestead in time for your brother's birthday. I'm sure you'll feel better once you see them again." Victor stood up to go.

"Sh-t, Victor. I'm sorry..." Julian snapped back into reality. He'd meant to at least keep Victor some company, offer some pleasant conversation for the evening, and it had turned into this, whatever this was.

"It's OK. I know my place, and I'm fine with it." Victor waved his hand at him. "I'll start at six, after my morning coffee."

"Stop being fine with it!" Julian grabbed him by the hand. "Demand something from me. I'm an ass. I need directions!"

Victor looked at him, startled. Then he looked at his hand still being held by Julian, and the commendable calm crumbled in an instant. The hand Julian was holding started shaking until it seemed to become unbearable, and Victor yanked it loose and shook it in the air.

"D-don't..." He resorted to signing the rest, "take that away from me. I can't sign if you do that." He seemed shaken. Odd, considering how uncharacteristically chatty he'd been so far. Julian had fully assumed he was drunk and fine with it, seeing as he'd looked calmer than usual. But maybe not?

"Do you know why Mr Ballroth wanted to buy this place?" Victor asked out loud.

"Why would I care what the old codger wants it for?" What a peculiar thing to ask out of the blue. Julian stood up to take his glass to the sink.

"He wants to restore the old shoe shop." Victor followed him.

"Why?" Julian debated whether to refill the glass instead. He turned to look at Victor, who seemed to be waiting for his attention.

"Rhys's great aunt was a dear friend of his, and he'd even hinted at courting her after some signs she might respond favourably. But ultimately he was content with the friendship, and, afraid to ruin it, he never spoke of his true feelings. Now, every time he walks past, it pains him to see it's no longer a shoe shop and that he's missed his chance. He even said he knows it won't help to have the shoes there on display, but he's desperate for any reminder of what was good in his life before he lost her. That's not how I want to end up!

"So even if I have to sign my way through some of the words, and even if it's just a supper I prepare to show my caring, and even if you miss my messages, I'll keep trying so I know I've tried my best. And who knows, maybe I'll end up getting through to you one of these days, but I sure as hell won't be left with regrets."

"You're getting through to me loud and clear, though..."

"Am I?"

"I mean, I thought so..." Julian was no longer sure. What else was he missing? The man was in love with him. Wasn't that what this had always meant?

"You keep confusing this with me wanting something specific from you or you having to reciprocate my feelings." Victor swallowed. "You really don't have to; love is not an obligation. I'm fine with how things are even if you reject me, and that doesn't change how I feel about you."

"Honestly, that makes me wildly uncomfortable," Julian admitted. He couldn't recall any situation where he'd done anything to merit or deserve such loyalty. He'd only ever been selfish in Victor's company. How intensely frightening to think that Victor might eventually realise this and rescind his caring regardless of what he'd just said. Worse even, he might do that just as Julian was ready to admit to his feelings.

"Ah, I was afraid you might say that. But it's better you said that out loud rather than let me keep making you uncomfortable. I'll stay out of your way as much as possible. You don't have to worry about it. I think Rhys might be a wee bit disappointed, though."

"Uh, how so?"

"He was cheering me on before he left." Victor let out a strained chuckle. "You know how he is."

Julian was at a complete loss for words.

"Or do you?" Victor frowned. "I suppose you don't..."

"What the hell. What else have I missed?" Rhys, at least, had been so closely under his nose he should have caught a whiff of whatever Victor was referring to, but apparently, all of absolutely everything lay behind an enormous blind spot.

But as much as Julian was curious, he was also irked by how easily Victor had steered the conversation in another direction. Hadn't he just lumbered through a full speech about Mr Ballroth to stress the importance of relaying one's feelings before it was too late? To make sure Julian was absolutely clear on those feelings, right? If it was that important to him, why did he accept defeat so easily? Unless...

Julian rubbed the bridge of his nose.

"You can seem like such a well-versed person for someone so clumsy with words." He didn't know whether to be impressed or frustrated. "And I am too dense to grasp the hint without it being explicitly pointed out to me. You brought all that up for *me* to not be left with those regrets, didn't you?"

"Yes, that was— t-that was the part I had trouble with..." Victor admitted, abashed. "But never mind that. I misread the situation and made you uncomfortable. I'm sorry."

"You didn't misread anything. I am indeed no better than Mr Ballroth and risk pining over a bloody shoe shop, but..." Julian sighed. "It's hard to relay my feelings when I'm not sure what they are. I might need some more time to figure it out."

"So long as you don't wait until I've keeled over," Victor joked.

"It's not too late yet. If you're not tired and don't mind keeping me company, I'd like to stay up a while longer to see whether I can figure some of it out."

Victor blushed and cleared his throat.

"I wouldn't mind at all."

Chapter 15

Victor sipped his morning cup of coffee at the dining table and hummed a cheery tune despite the ongoing downpour outside. Julian was still asleep, which was not customary for him at this hour but understandable considering the time they'd turned in after their chat the night before.

Victor was feeling a touch drained himself, but the coffee helped, and he'd promised Rhys he'd make sure the inventory would be done on time.

Finished with the coffee and without waiting for Julian to turn up to make breakfast, Victor headed downstairs to prepare for when the delivery man would bring some of Julian's newest stock.

He lit the log burner not so much for warmth as to dry the excess humidity in the pharmacy. Then he ventured into the storage room at the back to collect a box of old things left behind by Rhys's great aunt.

Since the delivery man was yet to arrive, Victor arranged a small decorative display of a few of the cobbler's old tools and three pairs of shoes on the other side of the shelf from where Rhys had propped his consultation sign.

The shoes had likely not been meant for sale, and by the state of them, they looked like something Rhys's great aunt had worn herself. They were not in outright disrepair, though, so Victor was able to wipe them clean, treat the leather and restore them to a decent shine without much effort.

There was a familiar pair of heeled shoes at the back of the box. They brought a faint smile to Victor's lips, even if the situation at the time hadn't called for one. He left them where they were in case it was still a sore subject for Rhys.

The stock delivery arrived promptly at seven, just as Victor was done with his homage to the shoe shop. There was still no sound of Julian getting up to make breakfast, so after receiving the stock and checking everything was there as ordered, Victor returned upstairs to make it himself.

Julian probably wouldn't get too cross over it.

And even if he did, he'd likely forget all about it by lunch.

Victor was halfway done with the omelette when the man appeared from his room, wiping his glasses on a handkerchief. His forehead creased briefly when he noticed Victor, but, for now, no perpetual canyons formed due to the unsolicited breakfast assistance.

Instead, Julian washed the previous evening's dishes, boiled himself some water for a pot of tea and sat down to wait for it to brew.

Victor cleared his throat.

"I made enough for two..."

Julian poured his tea into a cup and turned to look. It took him a moment to realise this was intended as a question, but thankfully he seemed to catch its meaning without Victor having to elaborate.

"Oh, yes, of course I'll have some. I'd love to have some, thank you," he said. Then he stood up to grab another tea cup from the cupboard for Victor.

Ah, good. He was no longer insisting on cooking for himself. The prickly remnants of Victor's nerves disappeared, and he served breakfast.

"Damn, did I oversleep past the delivery?" Julian noticed the time and sprung to his feet. "Were you up? Did it arrive?"

"I took care of it." Victor handed him a fork, and he sat back down.

"Thank you. That was careless of me..."

"Did you not sleep well?"

"Oh, no, on the contrary, I slept like a rock for the few hours that were left in the night." He gave Victor a smile.

Victor dropped the spatula on the table.

He then tried to recover the spatula but dropped it on the floor instead. When he reached down to grab it, he hit his head on the edge of the table and had to pause for a moment to nurse the bump before he could confirm that what he'd seen had indeed been a smile and check whether it was still there.

Julian was no longer smiling, likely because he'd reached over to check whether Victor was all right.

Victor had a feeling he'd hit his head with quite a loud bang, but he was too rattled about the smile to assess the level of noise or the severity of his head injury.

He'd seen Julian smile on occasion, but he couldn't recall the man smiling *at* him. At least not like that.

That was the last of the inventory done. Julian yawned for the fifty-eleventh time. It wasn't as easy to bounce back after a scarce few hours of sleep.

He carried the last empty crate to the back and left his inventory ledger on his desk. Victor was waiting for him at the stairs. He'd not said a word since the morning's spatula incident.

Julian had missed his chance to make breakfast, they had opted to skip lunch and had had a paltry snack, and he wasn't sure where to conjure the energy to prepare supper. Victor looked about as enthusiastic about the prospect. Perhaps, since they had to catch a train in the morning, an early night might be in ord—

"If you have yet to pack, I can take care of supper while you do." Victor headed up the stairs.

Damn it, Julian grumbled inwardly, he'd forgotten all about packing. Maybe it wouldn't take as long if he skipped folding his clothes. After all, it wasn't as if he needed to fit much in his suitcase since they were only going to stay at Grovestead for a couple of days. Besides, Quin had a whole wardrobe full of clothes that fit him at his house... At... their house.

Julian cringed, but it didn't feel as bad as he'd anticipated. Maybe... Maybe it wouldn't hurt to acknowledge the place was likely as much his as it was Quin's? After all, comparing that decor with Quin's room upstairs, it was clear who'd made most of the design decisions.

No, it was still annoying.

"Julian?"

"Hmm? Oh. Yes, sounds good to me."

Victor turned to sign his question. "Is everything fine?"

"I'm just tired and looking forward to sleep."

"Too bad—" Victor covered his mouth, rubbed his beard and faced away to continue up the stairs.

"How so?" Julian followed him.

The man seemed to mull it over before he replied in his usual candid manner, "I've enjoyed having you all to myself, so I was hoping for a repeat of yesterday."

They'd spent it chatting, so hearing Victor say he'd enjoyed it was saying a lot. But, while it had been nice, it hadn't brought Julian any closer to knowing whether something besides friendship existed between them. He could acknowledge he cared about Victor enough to be worried how the man would take rejection, but the kind of attraction he had for Rhys and Quin didn't seem to be there. Nor did he feel an inclination to explore it any further.

Victor had said he'd be fine with it, but it didn't seem fair. Julian felt he owed the man to at least try... but doing it out of pity would ultimately benefit no one.

"Why are you looking so sad about it?" Victor sounded amused. "I have other things to do. You don't have to entertain me if you're not feeling up for it."

"No, it's all right..." Julian stifled his yawn. "What other things?"

"Things."

This sparked Julian's curiosity enough to shake off some of his sleepiness.

"Painting?"

"No."

What else did he do in his free time?

"Are you making something?"

"No."

"Well, don't just mention it casually if you're not going to tell me!"

Victor turned to look.

"I'd show you but it's complicated." The infuriating ass put on the kettle, more or less ignoring Julian's mounting frustration.

Having been in this situation so many times—annoyed by Victor's scarce output and apparent calm—Julian was even quicker to anger than usual. One would think it would have got easier with practice, but, instead, his reservoir of annoyance required less than a trickle overflow because it was small and rarely properly drained.

Victor glanced to look at him again.

"Sorry, am I getting on your nerves?"

"Yes!"

"Do you need an excuse to vent? I don't mind."

What sort of an asshole regularly needed to reduce another person to a garbage receptacle to manage everyday irritation?

At any rate, it was easy to blame Victor, but Julian's current mood was probably more accurately ascribed to fatigue. It always brought with it a vague, nagging feeling of discontent, and, for the same reason, it was usually difficult to suppress.

"No. I'll deal!" Julian tightened his fists and took a few deep but strained breaths. Damn if it didn't feel annoying to have to deal with these feelings always resurfacing. Not only was he getting angry again, he was getting angry at getting angry again.

"It's probably because you're pent up. It's been a week since Quin left and a few days without Rhys. Tea?" Victor took a cup from the cupboard.

A tiny muscle at the corner of Julian's eye promptly gave up under the stress and began to twitch.

"I'm not in the mood for bloody tea!" He was at the familiar cusp of wanting to stay calm and yearning for the excuse.

"Right." Victor set the cups and the teapot aside. "Do you want to ring Quin and vent on the phone?"

"Don't be stupid!" Julian rolled his eyes. "I'm not going to purposely ring someone just to yell at them!" Besides, he'd already vowed to treat Quin better…!

"Well, then vent to me." Victor shrugged.

"Didn't you have something else to do?!"

"It can wait." Victor turned to face him. "Truth be told, I've been a little worried. You haven't blown up properly since Quin left…"

"What?! Am I supposed to blow up every few days? Is it expected now? I spent over ten years not blowing up! I should bloody well manage a week!"

"That was different."

"How was it different?!"

"Rhys filled me in. Your mother had done some things to help you manage the temper and keep you from accidentally connecting to Justin, but a lot of that was undone last year—"

"Why the hell does everyone know more about me than I do?!" Julian grabbed one of the teacups and smashed it to a wall. It felt good. He was about to grab the other when Victor stopped him.

Julian glared at Victor. How dare he interrupt? How dare he not let Julian have this? He pushed the man away, grabbed the other cup and smashed it all the same.

He was about to take the teapot when Victor grabbed another hold of him.

"You might burn yourself."

"Let me fucking burn—!" Before Julian was done with his sentence, Victor had detained him between himself and the wall.

"No." Victor's aggravating, persisting calm and difficult to read blank expression did not falter. Julian wanted to retaliate, but Victor's grip faltered even less.

Ah, Guardian damn it! Why wasn't Quin here? Quin would have known how to make use of this and make it stop—!

"Let go of me!" Julian struggled to get loose. He was further incensed and dismayed when Victor didn't let go immediately.

"Will you throw the pot if I do?"

"Yes!"

"All right," he said as if agreeing to it, but the man made no move to let Julian go. In fact, he leaned in, applied some more pressure on Julian's wrists and pinned one leg with a knee so he really could not move more than the other leg. In this strange position, he couldn't even kick the man properly.

"What is this, a sick power trip? Unhand me at once!"

"No. You'll hurt yourself."

"I swear to God, if you don't let me go, I'll—!"

"I'll let you go when you've calmed down."

"You know what, Victor? This will never work. I hate you! You're so full of yourself! You're such an annoying, timid piece of—!"

Victor simply watched him rave, which made the man seem even more infuriating. Julian was getting so riled up that for a split second, he wondered if this was enough to make his skull collapse into itself.

For several days now he'd been trying to figure himself out for Victor's sake to see if there could be something there, but all it ever amounted to was frustration. There was absolutely no chemistry there, no matter how much he wished for it.

Why the hell was the man so fine with everything? Why didn't he fight for it? That slight stutter, the embarrassed looks and all that indecisive waffling...! He would not speak for hours and then say elaborate, kind, thoughtful things like it was nothing, yet he couldn't take the initiative at all!

"Your wimpy-ass face makes my dick so damn depressed it's gone eternally limp because of you!" He was a fool for even thinking he could stray away from his preferred type. He was shallow to the core. It needed to be Rhys or Quin or nothing. "Say something!"

Victor merely watched him. Was there really nothing that could get a rise from the man? Julian was reduced to incomprehensible growls as he tried to jerk himself loose from Victor's grip.

CHAPTER 16

Some ten maybe fifteen minutes of struggling later, Julian had lost sight of why he was angry. Presumably it was Victor, but after calling the man every offensive thing he could think of, it had stopped making any sense even to him.

"Why the fuck aren't you saying anything?!" Julian's voice had gone raspy from the senseless yelling.

"It's taking you a little longer to calm down without Rhys or Quin here, but the tea has probably already gone cold, so I don't mind waiting." Victor sounded his usual self even after Julian's abusive tirade.

Julian clenched his teeth. How long was he going to keep him pinned to the wall? What the hell kind of strength did he possess to be doing it for so long and so effortlessly when Julian continued to fight him with all he had?

Victor lowered him down enough for his feet to touch the ground again.

"Are you done now?" He kept pinning Julian to the wall with one hand holding a wrist and the other now pressing across Julian's chest. Julian had a hand free, but he'd long since realised it made no difference.

"I don't think it's going to work out..." He'd been spewing obscenities, but at the heart of it, it wasn't so much the anger but the fear of disappointing Victor that fuelled it.

"Are you sure?"

"What the hell? Of course I'm su—hngh."

Victor had pressed his thigh to Julian's crotch. Julian would have looked down had he not still been pinned to the wall and unable to. Something was off... or unexpectedly *on,* to be precise.

The anger was promptly replaced by confusion as Julian wrestled with the momentary mind-body disconnect.

Oh, dear.

Shit.

Oh, Guardian all mighty.

Was it really...? It was, wasn't it?

Holy Sweet Mother of—!

Victor loosened his grip.

"Why? Why did you let go?" Just when it was about to get interesting!

"You're no longer angry."

"But..." Julian felt unstable on his feet, so he leaned on the wall to stay upright.

"What?" Victor moved his thigh away.

"But I..."

"Did you want something?"

How could he still be so calm? He sounded like he was about to offer Julian some tea!

Victor reapplied the hold. Ah, that was better. Julian relaxed. Victor let go of him again.

"Huh?" Was he taking a piss now? Who the hell was this man, toying with him like this when he was finally feeling willing...? Victor smiled. After all that, he had the gall to smile!

"Are you or are you not getting angry?" The forearm returned to hold Julian still. The relief was immediate.

"Did you fucking break me...?" What else could it be? He must have lost his mind, but lord, the pressure was comforting. It made his anxious tension melt away in an instant.

"Do you want me to do something?" Victor's question triggered a few disjointed wishes Julian wasn't sure how to articulate. His insides felt hot. "Press a little harder," he tried.

Victor leaned on him. He was heavy. Securely fastened to the wall, Julian felt much better again.

"Could you...?" Julian swallowed.

Victor pressed his thigh back to where it had been but this time Julian was fully aware of it. He was more than aware of what was underneath it.

"You need only ask," Victor said right by Julian's ear. Rumbly voice lowered to a whisper, he added, "but you need to ask."

T he gamble seemed to have paid off. Victor watched Julian squirm confused, but this being so outside Julian's usual character made it unexpectedly exciting.

After Victor had less than subtly made the man aware of his boner, the tide had turned and Julian had been reduced to a heap of butter, easy to mould.

"Would you like me to kiss you?" Victor asked. He'd forgotten his nerves at the sight of Julian looking like he was genuinely yearning for this. The sharp anger was beautiful, but this submissive side intrigued Victor on a whole new level.

Did he make this face with Rhys? Or Quin? Had he let anyone see himself like this, eyes so soft with longing? He seemed too prideful to ask for the kiss, but to Victor's surprise, he was trying to mouth something affirmative, even if no sound came out.

Victor couldn't resist a chuckle. Julian's annoyance was back, but it waned away as soon as Victor tightened his hold.

"I know how difficult it can be, but I'm going to need you to say it. Out loud." Victor leaned closer.

"Yes." Julian's eyebrows twisted into an unfamiliar angle. Victor was glad. This didn't seem the usual uncomfortable effort to agree out of pity. It seemed more like an invitation for some tongue. "Don't just ogle me. Do it."

Victor was still chuckling as he kissed Julian. How much happier could he have been? The man was even responding to the kiss!

"Ah, stop smirking. I think I need you to do something more." Julian even sounded breathy and, dare he say it, aroused.

"I can't help it. Let me enjoy this a while longer." Victor kissed him again. It had been magical the first time, but there had been a tinge of sadness believing it would never happen again. This time there were no interruptions and no audience. This time he could take his time and savour it.

"Ahhh... How are you this good?" The creases on Julian's forehead were gone. He'd relaxed and his eyes had melted even a degree further from soft to mellow.

"You flatter me." Victor smiled. "I like it."

It was Julian's turn to laugh, but he didn't sound happy. "I'm sorry I said such shitty things to you..."

"It's fine. I guessed you didn't mean them."

"No, I meant them. Almost all of them... You can grate me like no one else when I need to blow off some steam."

"Not even Quin?"

"Will you restrain me and fuck me if I say yes...?" The way Julian looked at Victor then was downright indecent.

"Do you want me to?"

"Yes."

"In that case..." Victor scooped him up to carry him to bed. Julian wasn't quite as easy to lift as Quin, and it wasn't precisely graceful, but it was likely quicker than to have him scramble there unassisted after all the energy he'd spent raging.

"Put me down! I can walk!"

The idiot was carrying Julian into bed, but Julian was too tired to put up a proper fight.

Victor climbed on top of him on the bed. He was presenting a good bit of assertiveness now, and the gentleness in his kisses was gone. He'd started unbuttoning the first two buttons of Julian's shirt but lost patience and ripped the rest of them off.

"Ahhhh...!"

Victor swept his tongue across Julian's abdomen, over his nipple and to the side of his neck. He traced the trail with his fingers, and when Julian instinctively tried to get up, he felt himself be pushed comfortably back against the mattress.

Maybe it was the experience with Rhys that made this feel so good? Or maybe he'd been into it all along...

The rougher Victor was, the better. Julian wished the man had become upset enough by the name calling to use some force, but taunting him further didn't seem right.

"Oh, uh? What's this?" It only then dawned on Julian what he was dealing with.

Victor's cock was inhumanely large! Was that even real? Julian swore. His first thought was to wonder whether this was what Rhys would have preferred and whether he'd known about it when he'd asked Victor to move in.

These were ridiculous thoughts, but they made his insides turn cold as he stared at it when it came into view.

The more immediate worry was for the safety of his orifices as that thing would not fit any of them.

It was impressive, though.

Julian found himself wondering whether it could have perhaps fit dreamside...

"It's not going to fit." What a sobering thought, but even more sobering was the realisation he would have otherwise been ready to let Victor give it a go without a second thought.

"I know. Don't worry." Victor kissed him to assure him.

If he and Quin had already done it, had Quin been able to accommodate something that size...? Shit, that thing was huge. The only way Julian could take his eyes off of it was to stare at Victor's face for any signs he might try something regardless of his assurances.

Victor pulled Julian's trousers down just enough to reveal the still dapper boner that hadn't cowered in the face of its stunning counterpart. Julian would have assumed these distracting comparisons would have done something to dampen it, but evidently Victor had managed to break him for good. So well, in fact, that he couldn't tell up from down anymore: it all felt both dreadful and exciting at the same time.

Victor produced a familiar bottle from his pocket and proceeded to massage the cool petroleum jelly onto Julian's dick until Julian was no longer able to form a straight thought.

Then that massive, hard cock was pressed against his and Victor massaged them both until Julian could form no thoughts at all.

He kissed Victor greedily. When Victor forced him to release to take a breather, he could not suppress his grunts and moans.

If he could have taken that thing in, he would have!

"Ahhhh!" Well, that was not a sentence to explain the sentiment. "Ahggnnnnnn... Ah... Ah..." Nor was that.

Victor paused for a moment. Julian tried to sign it since his mouth was too preoccupied to come up with the right words.

Victor smiled.

"I love you," he whispered into Julian's ear. He added some more jelly and adjusted himself. Julian had just enough time to scream inwardly when Victor gave it a thrust.

To Julian's surprise, it didn't hurt at all. The thing throbbed between his thighs and slid easily with the aid of the jelly. Victor's hand was still fondling Julian's shaft and glans, although not quite as deftly as before.

The beard was nowhere near thick enough to disguise Victor's face as he closed his eyes and thrust again. His bland features that had failed to awaken much in Julian before now turned his insides into liquid honey.

Julian was pinned under Victor's full weight for the moment the man moved his free hand to Julian's chin to hold it while they kissed.

"Ah... Haah..." Julian pushed the face away to look at it as it twisted from the pleasure. This was going to be difficult to unsee, but he could not resist watching Victor come. The man pushed himself up some ways and pulled out in time for his sperm to spray on Julian.

Julian could not decide which looked hotter, the monstrous cock against his own, with warm cum dripping all over them both and on his abdomen, or Victor's face as he convulsed from the pleasure.

The sperm made Victor's grip slip and slide as he made a brave effort to keep rubbing Julian off whilst distracted.

Julian could take no more of it and released his load.

When Victor recovered from his orgasm, Julian looked ready to pass out. He must have been exhausted. It had been a good choice to carry the man into bed to let him rest undisturbed the way he seemed. He had his hands outstretched to Victor's neck, and he was still watching Victor's face through the thin slivers of his nearly closed eyes.

Victor gave him a kiss.

"I love you, but please let me sleep..." Julian mumbled. Victor humphed, amused.

"You haven't packed yet."

This brought back the creases on his brow. Victor lay down next to him and tried to get them to ease by gently stroking his forehead and giving him another kiss. This seemed to do the trick. He closed his eyes.

"I'll do it for you," Victor whispered.

Julian let out a sigh like he'd been barely holding onto something. All that pent up tension and effort must have really sucked the juices out of him. Thankfully, this time Victor hadn't run out of time to say the things he'd wanted to say.

"I love you." He made sure to say it one more time, even if it looked like Julian might no longer be awake. The man responded with another sleepy, and this time incoherent, mumble.

He looked peaceful. Victor watched him sleep for a fair while but then got packing.

The train ride to Grovestead was its usual two-day ordeal, but for whatever reason, Julian felt well-rested and almost chipper when they arrived.

Chipper by Julian's standards was feeling such mild perpetual discontent that he was only periodically reminded of its existence when there were no distractions. It was overshadowed by an equally mild nervousness at the back of his mind when he thought about seeing Rhys and Quin again. Mostly, though, he felt fine.

There was no lingering strangeness between himself and Victor, who, like an absolute rock, was behaving just as he always did. Nothing suggested he had developed any unnecessary expectations. He was his usual self, albeit perhaps a tiny bit more relaxed around Julian.

The man offered to carry all the luggage since there wasn't much, but Julian took his suitcase and disembarked the train.

He was greeted by a gentle floral breeze that whisked away the stuffy smoky smell of the train. Quin had sent a carriage to pick them up from the station though the distance was mere minutes even on foot.

Seeing the mansion across the yard for the first time since last year, Julian enjoyed the subtle familiarity without its usual frightening undertone.

There was nothing to be afraid of here. If he lost his temper, it was likely not going to be anything too unmanageable, and he was among friends who would help him deal with it.

"Are you ready?" Victor took down the luggage from the luggage rack and offered Julian his suitcase. The staff hadn't sprung out to greet them like before, but they were probably busy with Vincent's birthday preparations.

"Yes. Let's get this over with."

Julian expected to have to deal with some extra enthusiasm from Quin after a whole week apart. While the added attention was annoying, it admittedly felt good to have been missed. Rhys would probably be less inclined to show something like that, so having Quin be his usual smarmy self was actually something Julian was looking forward to.

Julian knocked on the door. There was no response.

"You don't suppose they're already expecting Vincent, do you?"

Victor shrugged.

"It's just us!" Julian called out in case there were people waiting to surprise Vincent when he opened the door.

The entrance hall was empty.

"Ah, good. There's no one—" Julian turned to relay the good news to Victor.

"Surprise!" The dizzying array of voices echoed in the hall as people started to flood in through the three doors on the first floor and even through some of the doors upstairs in the mezzanine.

Ah, damn. What an impressive number of people they had managed to gather around for Vincent at such short notice! Julian noticed Rhys walking towards him from the side.

"I'm sorry, it's just me..." Julian felt incredibly guilty for having caused trouble.

"Happy Belated Birthday, Julian," Rhys seemed to be mouthing, his words inaudible over the cacophony of voices.

Julian spun to look through the unfamiliar faces of the crowd and felt his chest tighten from dread. He recognised his family, Mr Williams, Quin's two Nishkan associates and Quin in the approaching crowd, but who the hell were all these other rambunctious smiling faces coming at him? There were dozens of them!

"Don't be mad." Rhys took Julian by the hand and massaged it soothingly.

"Who are these people?" Julian was forced to ask. If they were here for him, how many of them were here to demand recompense or an apology for something he couldn't remember? He gripped Rhys's hand tighter than he'd intended.

"My name is Conrad Billows. Don't worry, Quin has already explained the situation. We used to go to school together. I came to wish you a Happy Birthday." The man in front of Julian hesitated briefly but gave Julian a quick handshake and a side hug. "I've missed you, friend. I'm glad to see you're doing all right!"

Quin cut through the line of people to give Julian a tight hug and a kiss on the side of his neck.

"Relax. They come in peace. Happy Birthday, Jules." Quin took Julian's other hand and squeezed it.

The sea of strangers looked just as menacing despite their cheerful expressions. Guest after guest came forth with happy introductions and explanations of where they knew Julian from, and they were all explicitly telling him how glad they were to see him.

Once they had been given a chance to give their congratulations, Quin announced it was time for Julian's guests to retreat to the back garden, while the remaining handful that were there for both Julian and Vincent reassumed their positions.

Rhys pulled Julian through the side door to hide.

"Vincent should be here at any moment. I heard from the butler that he was just spotted parking his turd mobile." Rhys peeked out the window to the front yard. The room he'd pulled Julian into had a handful of other people waiting—presumably guests here for Vincent.

Not that it was a competition, but didn't it seem like there were fewer than the crowd who had retreated into the back garden? But maybe the other rooms held more people and the distribution was off...

"How was your trip?" Rhys pried him from his thoughts.

"It was fine... Uh, did I leave my suitcase?"

"They've been taken care of," Victor said.

Rhys let go of Julian's hand to give Victor a hug. "How was it? Did you have fun?"

Julian found himself blushing. Thankfully, Rhys was not looking at him.

"Good," Victor replied. His response seemed to elicit some further excitement from Rhys, who gave the man another hug. Julian could have sworn he heard an almost silent congratulations just before Victor cleared his throat. Then they were interrupted by the sound of the front door.

"Now," Rhys gave the sign, and everyone rushed back into the entrance hall.

Vincent almost had a heart attack. He took a few steps back and bumped into Aurora, who graciously helped him stay upright. Oh, all the highest praises to the Guardian, he'd not succumbed to the craving to give Aurora a lengthy smooch at the door before entering, with all of these people waiting and potentially also peeking through the windows!

Celandine was already eyeing him suspiciously for leaning half on top of Aurora, so he straightened himself hastily and started to greet the onslaught of people pouring into the room.

"Ah, pardon my interruption!" Mr Quin shouted over the bustle, halfway up the stairs. "The dinner will be served in the back garden shortly. Please take your time here, but when you are ready, exit through those doors." He gestured at the double doors leading through another hall and to the garden. Then he excused himself, presumably to entertain the guests who appeared to already have made their way out to the back.

"Did you know about this?" Vincent asked Aurora, who nodded. How the hell had they managed this? Weren't the Brambles supposed to be in Herring Cove? And how the hell had they known to invite so many of his penpals, some even from overseas? Was that Mr Foxwick-Benton? Had they all come all this way for him?

Vincent realised Aurora had taken him by the arm and looked at him worried. When the tears fell on his cheeks, he realised he'd been welling up. Oh. Hah. He wiped them with his hands and laughed.

"I'm just so glad you all came…" he managed to say before Aster jumped to give him a hug. Funny how the tears came up so much more easily these days, and funny how it didn't feel as bad to cry. "Thank you for coming."

"Of course! We wouldn't miss it." He wasn't sure who had said it, but the people around him were all chiming in and nodding in agreement.

All of these lovely people were here for him. They weren't fans, strangers or people who he'd merely met somewhere along the way. Each face was someone who knew him beyond just his reputation. They wouldn't have bothered to come if he hadn't left an impression in their lives. That was a lot for a mere hall boy whose job was to remain unseen.

"Holy shit on a stick, Vincent, you gargantuan blister on a balding rump of a goat!" Rhys's voice carried well over the crowd.

"What? What now?" Vincent braced for impact.

"When did this happen?!" Rhys glared at him whilst politely lifting up Aurora's hand.

Oh, right. Oops. Vincent scratched the back of his head.

"It's fairly recent…" he tried to explain.

"The phone has been invented!" Rhys shot him one last venomous look, shook his head and turned to congratulate Aurora.

Vincent glanced worriedly at Aster and Celandine. Aster seemed over-joyed but Celandine less so. This was not quite how he'd intended to let them know.

"Does Ren know at least?" Rhys asked him.

"Yes… yes, of course she does. She helped me choose the ring…" Vincent hoped Aurora wasn't too upset that this had ruined any plans she might have had for making an official announcement. But there was still her side of the family left to inform…

Unless.

Vincent did a quick check of the people around him. There was indeed a huddled group of six looking mortified at the back corner of the room. He hadn't even met them yet!

It was fine, it was fine, it was—

"I'm screwed, aren't I?" Vincent cleared his throat. He felt faint. He felt worse than faint. There was a man and a woman at the centre of that group and they did not look happy *at all*.

Aurora smiled, so it seemed she wasn't upset. But that man, presumably Aurora's father, looked at Vincent like he was mentally preparing to skewer Vincent's behind with a Nishkan whaling harpoon. Nothing less than murder shone from his eyes.

Hadn't he just made the worst of first impressions by bumbling and crying in front of everybody? No wonder Aurora's parents were this displeased with him. Even Celandine looked benign compared to the couple still staring at the fool who had snatched their daughter with no prior consent or consideration...

Vincent could scarcely breathe.

It's all right, Aurora assured him, but she wasn't the one being murdered by their glares.

"I-I... I'm so sorry..." He tried to address them from across the room. His heart was skipping several beats during the course of the minutes of relative silence that followed.

"Why didn't you tell me?" Aurora's mother broke the silence and stepped forth to chastise her daughter, clearly deeply hurt.

"This is unacceptable," Aurora's father rumbled as he followed his wife.

In just a minute, Vincent expected to be beaten to pulp by the honestly quite stocky and intimidating man approaching him.

"He only asked me the day before yesterday," Aurora explained and showed her mother the ring. At least he'd spent a decent sum on it, so they could not fault him for being too stingy for their daughter.

"I had *plans!*" Aurora's mother wailed but took her hand to admire the ring.

"Your mother had plans!" her father echoed, almost equally exasperated.

"I know. I'm sorry. But I've told you many times to not make plans on my account," Aurora told them gently.

"I should have known!" Her mother looked absolutely forlorn. "I was looking forward to it."

"She was looking forward to it!"

"I only have one daughter left unmarried, and I have been waiting for this day since you were born."

To emphasise his wife's words, Aurora's father eyed his daughter sternly. While giving her this speech, they had all but forgotten Vincent's existence, but Vincent still struggled to breathe quiet enough to not to draw their attention.

"And how many times have I told you not to expect anything? You should be glad I'm getting married at all." Aurora didn't sound the least bit unnerved. "I did intend to give you a better introduction and more of a warning, but we've been busy. You know how it is."

"Yes, you are always so busy." Her mother sighed with conviction. "But at least I get to marry you off, right? This is just an engagement ring, isn't it?"

"Yes. We haven't set the date yet. I thought I would ask for your opinion—"

Aurora's words made her mother's face light up.

"Then all is not lost!" She grabbed her hands to shake them up and down with abundant enthusiasm. "May we still use my plans for the wedding?"

Aurora gave her the look Vincent had seen on occasion when he'd inadvertently said something stupid.

"*Some* of my plans?" her mother amended.

"I will take a look at them, but I'm making no promises. I want Vincent to also have a say."

The eyes returned to Vincent, and this time one pair shone brightly as if she'd seen the deity herself, and the other eyed him from head to toe as if inspecting cattle.

Vincent would have preferred to not have a say, quite frankly, if it had made the two of them happier with him.

"Happy Birthday, Mr Vincent," Mrs Vesper said. "And thank you for accepting our wayward daughter. My deepest apologies that she has chosen to become a doctor. I regret I wasn't able to dissuade her." This made Celandine, who stood not far behind Aurora's parents, raise her eyebrows. Perhaps the two of them would hit it off, lamenting and bonding over the supposedly detrimental career choice.

"That's one of the things I like about her, though..." Vincent said weakly, wary that his words might still render him the target of more murderous glares. Mrs Vesper seemed no longer so inclined and shook his hand instead. Perhaps because she had calmed down, her husband followed suit.

"There. Since that's settled for now, can we find somewhere for Vincent to sit for a while? He's been on his feet or driving all day," Aurora said.

"I'm fine."

"You're hardly bearing any weight on it."

Ah. Vincent changed his footing but had to admit it was starting to feel uncomfortable. How did she always notice these things so quickly?

There's no use trying to disguise it. I've already noticed. She looked at him and took his hand to guide him through the crowd.

"Let's find us some seats, and you can all take turns congratulating him when he's off his feet!"

Vincent squeezed Aurora's hand and let her lead.

Hosta stood alone at a distance and watched the party guests mingle and chatter. Bits and pieces were still missing from her memory. Possibly more than she was aware of, but what she remembered was enough to make sense of the overall sequence.

It left her with an inexplicable feeling of calm seeing her two eldest sons celebrate their birthdays among such a plentiful crowd of guests.

Vincent looked well-rested and happy. Julian was surrounded by people practically doting on him despite him occasionally barking at them. Even when it looked like he was on the verge of completely losing his temper, his friends reacted to it with a casual ease she couldn't have imagined possible, and it was yet to escalate beyond manageable.

All of these people were here for her sons as testament that they were capable of forming the meaningful relationships she'd feared would be unattainable for them. What more could a mother hope for?

She retreated from the garden, assured that they would be fine without her.

CHAPTER 18

The guest rooms had all been allocated even after most of the guests had left for their homes at the tailend of the evening. Those that had come from afar had a place to stay here so no one was forced to cut their evening short just to find a place to stay for the night. There were still a fair number of people in the back garden enjoying each other's company and snacks and drinks by the bonfire.

Some of Julian and Quin's mutual acquaintances were a little on the rowdy side, although in merry spirits and successfully containing their rowdiness to their particular cluster at one end of the garden. A few of Vincent's more adventurous guests had joined them, and the rest still up at this hour had formed another slightly calmer group at the tables where the dinner had been served.

Rhys was sitting next to Vincent, who was recounting one of his stories to the rest of the guests around his table without showing any signs of being inconvenienced by their nearly nonstop requests. Rhys had already heard this story many times before, so he was distracted, watching Julian and Quin at the other end of the garden amidst what seemed like lively conversation.

Julian seemed to be enjoying himself.

Rhys had been waiting for a pang of jealousy to hit over the two of them getting along so splendidly, but he was yet to feel anything but contentedness. They seemed to be in a bubble of their own, with a shared past and a circle of friends Rhys was not a part of. Neither of them had so much as glanced at Rhys at the other end of the garden for over an hour, and all Rhys felt was immensely relieved that they were enjoying themselves.

Julian wasn't hugely into public displays of affection, but he was clearly drunk and practically hitched to Quin, whose confident smiles were absolutely radiant tonight. The two of them would greet each other with their tongues whenever they looked at each other.

Rhys chuckled. Maybe he was so fine with it because, when he'd walked over there a little over an hour ago to ask how they were doing, they had *both* tried to greet him with those tongues, the drunken bastards. Maybe it was because watching them interact kept warming up Rhys's insides as if he'd been either of them himself. What sense was there to be jealous?

But as much as he was enjoying the view, Rhys couldn't keep stifling his yawns forever. It was getting late.

He looked over to the far side of the table to see whether Victor was still around, and, as it happened, the man seemed to be about to take his leave.

"Excuse me, I think it's time I retire," Rhys said to Vincent and stood up to go.

"Ah, yes..." Vincent, who had already been on his feet to tell his story, scooped Rhys into a tight hug. "Thank you for the party; for everything." He gave Rhys a sheepish smile.

"It was my pleasure." Rhys patted his shoulder. "But I think you ought to sit down before she chews your head for straining the knee."

Aurora raised her brow. Vincent turned to look at her and sat down hastily.

Rhys excused himself and hurried to follow Victor who had already headed inside but whose towering figure could still be seen through one of the windows.

With the house filled to capacity, Quin had suggested the four of them share his and Julian's rooms. Having guessed that Julian and Quin might want to refresh old memories, especially if they dipped slightly more heavily into their drinks, Rhys had agreed it was likely wisest to let the two of them take Julian's room while Rhys and Victor bunked in Quin's.

Victor was already at the top of the stairs when Rhys caught up with him.

"Oh, hello." The man looked a tad confused to see Rhys. "You're retiring already?"

"Yeah, I thought I might. But if you're not tired, I wouldn't mind hearing how your week went." On the off chance that the view in the garden hadn't been as much of a pleasure for Victor, perhaps a reminder of the presumably enjoyable week with Julian would cheer him up.

Victor stopped at the door to Quin's room and opened it for Rhys. The room was similar to Julian's, although something about the lush, rich fabrics and smooth finishes of the decor made Rhys feel oddly like his senses were being shamelessly pampered with luxury. He headed for a chair by one of the large windows, planted his knees into it and looked over the backrest and out into the garden.

"It's a lovely view," he mumbled. His mind wandered to the moment later in the night when the view would make its way into the room next door.

Victor did not respond. He seemed to be changing into something more comfortable.

"Do you mind sharing the bed?" Rhys asked, took off his waistcoat and tossed it aside somewhere.

Quin had said to ask the staff to bring in a second bed, but amidst all the other arrangements, Rhys had forgotten all about it. Quin's was a ridiculously wide four-poster bed, so it didn't seem like a problem to share it even with someone Victor's size.

"No. Not if you don't." Victor folded and set his dress clothes neatly on a bench and sat on the side of the bed already in his nightshirt.

"So, tell me all about it. How was it?" Rhys perked up and jumped to sit cross-legged on the bed, almost ripping a seam of his trousers in the process. He readjusted and started shuffling the stupid things off. Victor seemed to be waiting for him to be done with it. Either that, or he was nervous despite not looking like he was.

Rhys made himself comfortable on top of the duvet and watched the needlessly fancy rolls of fabric that cascaded down from the bed crown somewhere above him.

"How much detail do you want?" Victor's relaxed voice rumbled in the otherwise silent room. Somewhere far off, the muffled sounds of Julian and Quin's friends were still audible but far from anything that would disturb anyone's sleep.

"All of it." Rhys requested briskly. The moment he'd said it out loud, something within him shifted a gear into reverse, and he realised how bold his request was.

Damn it. He glanced at Victor, who was still sitting at the side of the bed but turned so his side profile was visible. The man seemed unperturbed.

It was still no less annoying to realise that his slender physique had yet again failed him and that the wine had done him in worse than he'd realised. He'd observed the others getting tipsy and privately chuckled at their drunk antics... and here he was, blurting out things he'd not meant to bring to anyone's attention.

Victor turned to look at him.

"Ah, no, I didn't mean... You don't have to tell me. Not like *all* of it obviously. Just the general, you know... I don't mean to pry. I'm a little drunk, obviously..." A blush made its way to Rhys's cheeks, and he groaned inwardly.

"I'll tell you if you really want to know." Victor shrugged.

Fuck. That was worse. Rhys's imagination kicked into gear as if reverse had never existed. What was *all* of it? What had they done? Something similar as with Rhys? Or like with Quin? He realised his heart was pounding, and was that a hint of sweat on his palms...? He hastily wiped them on the duvet.

All of a sudden, lying on his back felt intensely uncomfortable, so he sat up and hugged his knees.

"You don't have to be shy about it, Rhys." The good thing about Victor and Victor's face was that it always looked largely the same, and it seemed thankfully devoid of judgement now. Rhys couldn't quite let go of the embarrassment, though, so he hid his face. "I know," the man added.

What do you know? Rhys peeked from behind the knees and forearm he'd shielded himself with.

"I saw you watching them."

Shit. Was it that obvious? What had he seen? Rhys struggled to breathe.

Victor chuckled. "I'm not quite as keen to watch, but I can see the fascination."

"Was it really that obvious?" Rhys sighed, dejected. Had he unwittingly made a fool of himself out there?

"I don't think anyone else was paying much attention to it; don't worry." It was Victor's turn to lie back and make himself more comfortable. "I only noticed because I was a little worried about you."

"What did I do?" Rhys frowned. He'd been busy making sure everything was going smoothly so that Quin could relax and have a nice time with Julian.

"Let's just say I would have pulled you away from the table with me had you not slowed down with the drinks on your own after you got back from checking up on them. Were you worried?"

"About what?" Hearing Victor's view of the evening made Rhys even further embarrassed.

"That they might not get along. Or that they might forget you."

With the way the both of them had gravitated towards Rhys when he'd popped to see them, it was difficult to imagine them ever forgetting him. But he had admittedly been a little worried about whether Julian might drink himself sick. There was also always the possibility of him connecting to Justin or Quin riling him up on purpose in front of the guests... In hindsight, the crowd that had remained at the back of the garden after dinner had been rough-seeming but comradely enough to not mind such things. And even if Julian did connect to Justin or drank excessively, Quin would probably take good care of him. In any case, none of it was worth him carelessly drinking himself silly.

"I promised Hosta I would keep an eye on Julian's drinking, but, since Quin was already glued to him, I left that up to him and took over his hosting duties. I guess I got a little distracted. I didn't even realise…"

"I know. Sorry. That was a bit of a crude joke," Victor admitted then. "It was sweet how you watched over them and made sure they have a nice evening with all their old friends here. You joining all the toasts with both Vincent's tables and the back garden posse concerned me, though, but thankfully you didn't stick around back there for too long and Vincent was quick enough to get the stories going before you hurt yourself trying to match everyone. I was surprised you retired so early, though, since you looked like you enjoyed watching the two of them… Did curiosity get the better of you?"

"I—"

"I cooked Julian supper. We talked almost through the night. He was still on edge the following day, so I gave him an opportunity to vent." As Victor continued with his account, Rhys clutched on the duvet, mind blank of anything else but the disturbingly vivid mental images conjured up by Victor's words.

Two hard cocks rubbing against one another, dripping cum all over Julian's abdomen.

Rhys had expected something but he hadn't quite prepared for this amount of juicy details relayed by a narrator whose bass could massage his insides even without the luscious subject matter. Sweat pearled at the back of his neck, and he swallowed. "I— I think I need a wee…" He jumped off the bed and scurried out of the room. It was not a lie, but he praised the timing.

U nfortunately, even after dallying to fetch half a bottle of port from the wine cellar after he'd done his business, Rhys found his uncomfortably observant and talkative roommate still awake in Quin's room, but at least he'd managed to mostly recover from hearing the man's tale…

"A nightcap?" Rhys offered, hoping Victor was kind enough to not bring up the previous subject.

"Sure."

Rhys poured them both a glass and set the bottle aside. He'd just taken a sip when Victor resumed with, "So, all of it, was it? Even my encounter with Quin?" and made him almost expel his drink through his nose.

"With Quin?!"

"Yes, after we busted through your door. I'm sorry about that by the way. We didn't mean to disturb you."

"Oh." Rhys gripped the glass of port and stared into it. Quin and Victor… that seemed like it might be interesting. Damn it. He took a hasty swig from his glass.

"And a few times after that. Or rather, every time he's had trouble sleeping. But I don't mind entertaining him, since he's always so appreciative of the attention."

Rhys could just about imagine what Victor was referring to. It was one of the reasons why watching Quin and Julian together was so rewarding.

"He's deliciously sensitive," Rhys thought out loud. Victor glanced at him but said nothing. "I may have... *entertained* him, as you put it, myself a few times." He'd sworn to keep his hands off since Agnes Point because Quin seemed like he might start obsessing if he was given the slightest bit of something to obsess about, but the man was so damn 'appreciative', it was hard not to mess with him whenever the opportunity arose.

Victor lifted his hands to sign, "Would you like to watch me do him sometime?"

Rhys was still staring intently into his glass, but he'd clearly not missed Victor's signs the way his cheeks had turned red and he seemed to have trouble breathing.

"You'd like that, right?" Victor couldn't resist confirming out loud. "You'd like to watch me play with him until his dick weeps, and he's moaning and begging for release." Not an easy string of words to put together, but he'd had good practice while recounting the details of his evening with Julian, and this was so worth it to see Rhys's brow crease in intense concentration as he was likely imagining it and trying not to give away how aroused it was making him—again.

He probably thought he was doing a decent job at disguising it, but he looked just about as bothered as he had when he'd heard about what had happened with Julian.

Then again, Rhys had been casting longing eyes at Julian and Quin all evening, restless like a cat in heat, so he'd been well-primed to receive the few choice words. Victor pretended to ignore him so as not to scare him away like the last time he'd got a little too descriptive.

Rhys threw back the rest of his drink, but fortunately, while bigger than what one might normally use for port, he'd originally poured himself a modest half a glass. Victor took his glass away to put it on the nightstand and watched him not know what to do with his hands now that they were free.

He glanced at Victor with a troubled expression then signed with his hands shaky and signs barely legible, "You're talkative today."

"It's probably the wine," Victor mused. Although, it wasn't exactly enough to make this effortless. The bulk of the motivation was provided by his intriguingly receptive audience: he'd never imagined his voice and words could have this effect on someone. "Want to make some guesses as to what our neighbours will do when they finally turn in for the night? Do you want to stay up, wait and listen?"

W ho was this person lying in the bed next to him, Rhys thought as he struggled to adjust to Victor's unfettered and ample output.

"Just lie back and relax. I can entertain you with my guess while we wait," he was saying as if to make idle conversation.

Rhys was rendered speechless. He lay back and tried to relax. His head was becoming pleasantly muddled by the port, which was immensely helpful in taking the edge off of the embarrassment still heating his cheeks. But the downside was that he was a little too slow to decline Victor's offer, and the man obliged with another detailed account of what he supposed Julian would do to Quin when they arrived.

Was the cover on this duvet silk, or were his fingers playing tricks on him? Why was it so soft and smooth against his skin? Why was Victor's voice so warm and smooth, as if it, too, was caressing him all over? He'd meant to give Julian and Quin some privacy this evening, but it was starting to feel less and less like something he wanted to honour. If he'd been in this room alone when they arrived, he could have at least—

Quin guided Julian towards the door and opened it for him. The man was sloshed but not yet to the point of uselessness, and Quin was accustomed to dealing with his drunk ass since the days when he'd been much more messed up than mere wine could make him. He'd been getting weepier and more emotional, though, probably due to the connection to the Guardian acting up, so Quin had persuaded him to retire to save the others from his confusing moods.

Quin could vaguely recall something similar to this happening before, although usually Julian's response to it was to feed his anger, pick a fight and let that take care of it. He'd been much more subdued today, and it would have disturbed Quin more had he not known about Justin and the connective issues.

"We're in the room now," Julian pointed out to remind Quin of his promise to give him head once in private.

"This first." Quin poured him a glass of water from a pitcher he'd known to arrange for this very reason. Julian looked at him, strained, but gulped down the water. Quin rescued the glass from its unreliable grip and put it on a side table before cupping Julian's cheeks and kissing him.

"Make me feel better," the man slurred and pressed his forehead to Quin's.

"I will, I promise."

When Quin massaged the front of his trousers, Julian leaned back against the wall and relaxed under his touch. Quin had been looking forward to a rough night, but it didn't seem how this was shaping up to be. However, all the preparations and excitement leading up to the party had taken their toll on Quin, too, so he wasn't going to be overly cross if this ended with a blowjob or a quick fuck before spooning until morning.

The room next door had been suspiciously quiet since the return of its occupants. Victor strained to hear whether someone had really entered a few minutes ago or whether he'd imagined it.

"Oh, listen." He lifted a finger. "It's Julian," he signed the rest to not disturb Rhys when he was trying to listen.

"How can you tell?" Rhys signed back clumsily.

"I can tell," Victor whispered. "His voice becomes whiny when he's tired. Quin is probably giving him head."

It would probably never cease to entertain him how the normally so assertive and lively Rhys was reduced to biting his lip and holding his breath when a concept like this was introduced to him and he was flustered about it.

"Don't forget to breathe. Would you like me to go ask them if you can watch?"

"Ah—" Rhys shut his eyes as if the frustration had just become too painful for him to bear. Victor had said it to tease and felt a little guilty about it, but now that he'd said it, he wondered why it hadn't sounded like a half bad idea.

"Maybe they're trying to be considerate? I could at least tell them not to be." Funny how interrupting the two didn't make Victor at all as nervous as it should have. He wasn't as drunk as Rhys, so it wasn't the wine making him braver than usual. It just felt like a *safe* thing to suggest.

Rhys looked at him like he was under a spell: too shy to tell him yes but eyes pleading for him to take the hint.

Well, why not? Victor stood up and headed for the door between the two rooms. He gave it a polite knock and looked in.

"Hi, excuse me. Do you mind if Rhys comes to watch? He's been fantasising about it all day," Rhys heard Victor say.

"No!" Rhys was yanked out of the strange trance Victor's voice had put him in, and he bolted up and out of the bed.

"Is there a problem?" Victor was asking. He'd entered their room by the time Rhys scrambled to the door, panting. "Oh, put your forearm here and hold him still. That's probably enough..." Victor was instructing Quin when Rhys peeked into the room.

They had pinned Julian against the wall, although it was mostly Quin doing the holding. Victor turned to look at Rhys and gestured for him to come in. Rhys was too distracted to move.

None of his usual irritation was visible on his face, but Julian's expression looked eerily familiar. Rhys clutched to the door frame. The memory of Julian's dreamside feminine form flashed in Rhys's mind, and if he hadn't already been aroused from the prolonged tease Victor had staged for him, this would have been more than enough to do the job.

Julian reached to kiss Quin and Quin obliged. Victor stood behind Quin's back, and instead of retreating after he'd helped Quin to restrain Julian, he embraced him from behind, sandwiching him between himself and Julian.

Rhys felt weak in the knees. He'd entertained himself with thoughts of them fooling around respectively, but it had never occurred to him to imagine this happening at once. Was it really OK for him to stay and watch?

Quin had seemed level-headed a moment ago, but he'd assumed the form of a liquid when Victor had opened the front of his trousers, pulled him out and used the other hand to feel the front of his shirt to locate his nipple. Quin had got as far as pulling down Julian's trousers and underwear and was kissing the man, but he'd lost his concentration and forgotten what else he was supposed to do.

Rhys pried his eyes off of the scene by obstructing the view with a hand, but his resolve was only good for two seconds before he peeked again between his fingers.

Julian looked frustrated pinned where he was, eyebrows knitted and hands searching for something to grab. Rhys knew that look. Unfortunately, he had nothing to thrust into the hole the man currently did not have, even had he been where Quin stood.

"Quin... Quin...!" he tried to get Quin's attention. Quin let out a nasally hum while being kissed. It sounded like it might have been an acknowledgement that he'd heard. "QUIN!" Rhys tossed him the petroleum jelly from the nightstand not far in front of him.

It was Victor who caught it, glanced back and donned an expression of understanding. Good. This seemed to be going somewhere—

Oh, shit.

The noises slipping out of Quin's mouth when Victor lubed his dick made Rhys's insides so soft he almost fell to the floor. He clung onto the doorframe and bit his lip so hard he thought it might bleed.

Quin was still struggling to grasp the script, so, voice hoarse from his arousal, Rhys tried again to gain his attention.

"Quin, you idiot... Don't make him wait!"

"Huh?" Quin managed a sideward glance. He seemed to be making an effort to comprehend, bless him.

Victor eased with what he was doing so that Quin had a fighting chance to grasp the incredible prize dangling right in front of him. To be fair, it had probably never occurred to him he could be in this position. When the prospect dawned on him, he looked like he might cry, but, to his credit, he wasted no more time.

Victor helped him get Julian into a better position, but when the pieces aligned, Quin entered Julian, and shortly after, Victor copied him and pushed them both against the wall with a series of grunts.

Rhys closed his eyes and crouched down to his haunches, but there was no escaping the sounds that ensued—not unless he made a proper run for it. Even if he could have made his legs work, he wasn't going to leave when the maximum time he could bear without looking was the span of a few thrusts and moans.

After a while, it was like his brain had completely short-circuited. He stared at the three precious souls as their bodies joined together, touching and caressing one another in ways that he could vividly imagine the feel of thanks to the bond he had with each of them and the experiences they'd shared together. He didn't think he'd ever seen anything more beautiful. The only way this could have been better was if he wouldn't have had to blink at all.

CHAPTER 20

Julian felt the jumbled contents of his head realign as he ejaculated and the pleasure washed away some of the vague grief that kept resurfacing and souring his otherwise decent mood. He gifted Quin's lower lip with a few more bites and kisses, and from this distance, he could practically taste the man's heated moans. It didn't take many more thrusts for Quin to climax, although when he did, he shot Julian the sort of unfamiliar, greedy, almost angry look Julian wasn't sure he'd ever seen Quin direct at him before.

It was like he was upset at Julian for having an orgasm and consequently causing a supposedly premature chain reaction, as if Julian had had much choice in the matter. He'd hung on for as long as he could, but it was Victor's hand—! He turned to look over Quin's shoulder.

Victor was *biting* said shoulder, his eyes closed and brow furrowed. Quin's gaze grew bleary as he stood there, his full weight now supported by the two people he was wedged between and his body still spasming from his orgasm. Julian sensed the reason for the change in his expression as it wasn't just Quin's spasms he could feel with his body so firmly pressed against the wall by the two of them.

Victor released his bite and took some hungry breaths before opening his eyes to look back at Julian. Julian caught Quin, who barely hung on to him, heavy and breathless. Victor's cum dripped down Quin's inner thighs, and it reminded Julian of the sight of that cock dripping against his own. Ah, these two... What a wonderful combination.

"Can you stand?" Julian asked Quin. The man straightened himself up with some help from Victor behind him. Julian's own legs felt akin to jelly but that was less of a reason to fall over than the sway from all his drinking. It hadn't been as obvious when he'd been pushed against the wall, so he'd forgotten all about it.

"Can you...?" Quin looked at him worried and offered a hand for support. Julian had half a mind to take it but waved it away instead. His attention was gripped by something at the corner of his eye.

"Rhys?"

Oh, shit. Was he upset? Julian tried to make sense of that expression. Quin also turned to look.

"Oh, hi, Rhys." Quin waved at him. There was no discernible response to his greeting. Rhys was on his knees and seemed to be staring in a state of shock. "Is he all right?" Quin turned to ask Victor.

Victor didn't answer but walked over to Rhys, knelt down next to him and said a few words Julian couldn't quite make out. Rhys still looked unresponsive. Had it been that much of a shock for him? Julian was about to berate himself for being an idiot when Quin took his hand and pulled him along to go talk to the man.

"He's all right. I think," Victor told Quin.

"What's wrong?" Quin crouched down and gently lifted Rhys's chin up. A few tears rolled down his cheeks, and Quin wiped one with his thumb. "Did you feel left out?"

Rhys shook his head and faced away. He seemed to be breathing raggedly. Was he drunk? Or sick? It was Julian's turn to look closer.

Wait.

He emulated Quin and lifted Rhys's chin up to meet his eyes. Rhys looked back at him, confirming that there was something very familiar with his flustered cheeks and laboured breathing.

Oh.

Julian frowned.

"You should have just said something if you wanted to join us..."

"No." Rhys's voice was barely audible.

"But you're—"

"Don't say it." He seemed deeper into it than if he'd had a couple of fingers literally wiggling inside of him. It should have been obvious with a mere glance even from a distance, but to be fair, Julian hadn't expected it, and he wasn't at his most perceptive.

"Do you want some help with that?" Julian asked and glanced at both Quin and Victor. Rhys bit his lip and shook his head again. "Why not? We're not busy."

"**I** — Oh, fuck..." Rhys felt light-headed.

They were not busy.

Were *they all* going to help him out with this? Rhys had just about recovered from not breathing right and almost making himself pass out, and he was already overheating again from the thought of *them all* helping him.

Julian pulled him up to stand and gave him a hug. "I'll be up for it in just a minute. You know I'll always be up for it, for you..."

"Yeah, but—" Rhys felt himself hoisted off the ground. This time it was not just Julian doing the carrying but the three of them making an even lighter job of it. They lay him into Julian's bed, and Julian sat on one side and Quin and Victor on the other. Were they really all going to stick around for this? This was not dreamside—

Julian kissed him. It didn't take much to distract Rhys from his worries, and Julian had had a lot of practice. But no matter how aroused he was, it wasn't going to make Rhys's body look right, and even though Victor and Quin knew, would seeing it in the flesh change their minds about something?

Quin interrupted them by putting his hand on Julian's back.

"Jules, wait."

"Hmm?"

"Should we leave? I mean, me and Victor." He turned to Rhys. "I want you to be comfortable, and I can see you're not."

Victor nodded.

What a relief, honestly. Rhys might have even wanted Julian to excuse himself so he could have had a moment to deal with this alone... It was a little too intense to even think about the three of them in the same room right now.

Quin was twirling his fingers through Victor's hair. Were the two of them going to continue that in the next room...? A few choice lines within Victor's tale of their previous encounters started looping within Rhys's mind.

Shit. Why was he this wound up and unable to let it go? He wanted to see that, but there would be a wall in the way!

"S-stay."

"Are you sure?" Quin asked, but the single word had brought a wide grin to his face.

"Y-yes." As soon as Rhys had said it, Quin crawled over to him like an overjoyed puppy.

"May I join in? You can change your mind and kick me off whenever you want, but I'd like to. I like you. I love you. You're my second favourite person, tying with Victor. I'd like to return all of the favours!"

Rhys opened his mouth but couldn't form a response. He glanced at Victor. Victor looked back at him and signed the word 'same' and a question.

"F-fuck." Rhys slapped himself on both cheeks to force his brain to cooperate. Was it altogether too greedy to want all of them at once...? This amount of excitement could hardly be healthy for him.

But—as Quin would put it—the best things in life were, for the most part, unhealthy.

"Fuck me," he said.

GLOSSARY

May contain spoilers!

ARF mask, the (the Automated Rest Facilitator), A mask applied to a person to stop them from sleep-roaming and interfering with the Guardian's automated rest procedures.

Dreamside, the alternate state of reality that Rhys perceives when he sleeps.

Ear of the City, an affluent area of Schadesborough with a distinct style in architecture and a lot of immigrants from the North.

Furuyan, the name of the continent where this story takes place.

Guardian, supposedly a widely worshipped deity on Furuyan, second only to the god of another monotheist religion similar to Christianity. More accurately, an apparatus used for analysing, diagnosing, preventing and curing health issues related to, or through, sleep.

Learian Deerhound, a large, skinny breed of dog from the distant continent of Learysa.

Maury, (Holy Maury, Mother of the Sea and Weaver of the Waves) the deity most revered by the fisher communities in the Arctic regions of Furuyan.

Midwinter, a time of celebration during the winter solstice.

Nishkan whaling harpoon, something sharp and pointy you do not want to be skewered with.

Petroleum jelly, the least harmful substance one might use for intimate lubrication at the time. Not otherwise recommended.

ReM Clinic, the (the Restful Meadows sleep disorder research clinic), Hosta's sleep research clinic that burned down in Schadesborough.

Void, the unwelcoming space between the bubbles.

Whitskersey, the Island of the White Skerries, a small island in the Arctic, near the Crook of the Ear.

Cast of Characters

Billows, Conrad one of Julian and Quin's old friends.

Bramble, Arthur Aster and George's son.

Bramble, Aster George's wife, Vincent's guardian.

Bramble, George Aster's husband, Vincent's guardian.

Buttercup, Celandine Aster's sister, Vincent's guardian.

Craft, Jasmine Julian's younger sister.

Craft, Julian Rhys's pharmacist tenant.

Foxwick-Benton, Mr aka Mr Benton the brother of the former head of Benton House.

Hart, Victor Rhys's attic tenant.

Poppycock, Dr James Vincent's therapist.

Quin, Adair Julian's former partner in crime.

Steadfast, Edward Vincent's friend.

Swifty, ~~Mr~~ Sir Vincent's trusty feline companion.

Swifty, Ren Vincent's ward. Bryony and Marcus's daughter.

Swifty, Vincent the title character of the book. Ren's guardian.

Vesper, A.L. (Aurora, Vera) a doctor specialising in sleep science at the Sleepy Leighs Treatment Centre.

Vesper, Mr & Mrs Aurora's parents.

Wakefield, Rhys M. our building-owning protagonist.

Williams, Mr Julian's archaeologist friend.

About the Author

J.B. Thwaite is the author of dozens of best-selling books that only exist in her dreams. She lives in the darkest, most inhospitable depths of Southern Finland with her spouse, scion and feline companion. She has discovered fire and re-invented the wheel in exactly the same form as before but better. With an incredibly busy schedule, she uses her scarce free time to nap, sleep and doomscroll on social media. She is also a connoisseur of the highest quality Asian homoerotic literature and a bit too neurodivergent to enjoy long walks on the beach.

ALSO BY

The Catnap Ramblers:
Vincent and the Cat (2023)
Rhys and the Voiceless (2023)
Aurora and the Guardian (2023)

The Catnap Fumblers (extra novellas):
Private Afterwords (2024)
Solicitous Missteps (2024)

Other books in the works:
Pandion (2024)